"Do I m̶̶̶̶̶̶̶̶̶̶̶̶̶̶̶̶̶̶̶̶̶̶̶̶ced with a devilish gr̶̶̶̶

"It's not you, exactly," Heather said, her cheeks reddening as she turned away and began preparing the omelets. "It's—it's just the circumstances under which I invited you to dinner. I mean, I usually don't drag men out of half-empty apartments and bring them home with me."

"Look, maybe it would help if I told you that I'm—"

"Harmless? I'll bet you haven't been harmless since the day you were born. Oh, I'm being silly, acting like a schoolgirl. Just ignore me."

Jace laughed, and his voice deepened as he spoke again. "That would be a tough assignment, Heather." He began walking toward her and she felt her skin tingle as the distance between them narrowed. "In fact, it's totally impossible. I'm much more inclined to kiss you than ignore you," Jace said, cupping her face in his hands and lowering his head to hers.

"You are?" she said breathlessly as his lips began a gentle nibbling on her throat.

"I am," he said firmly, and pressed his lips to hers in a fiery embrace that stunned them both. . . .

WHAT ARE *LOVESWEPT* ROMANCES?

They are stories of true romance and touching emotion. We believe those two very important ingredients are constants in our highly sensual and very believable stories in the *LOVESWEPT* line. Our goal is to give you, the reader, stories of consistently high quality that may sometimes make you laugh, sometimes make you cry, but are always fresh and creative and contain many delightful surprises within their pages.

Most romance fans read an enormous number of books. Those they truly love, they keep. Others may be traded with friends and soon forgotten. We hope that each *LOVESWEPT* romance will be a treasure—a "keeper." We will always try to publish

LOVE STORIES YOU'LL NEVER FORGET
BY AUTHORS YOU'LL ALWAYS REMEMBER

The Editors

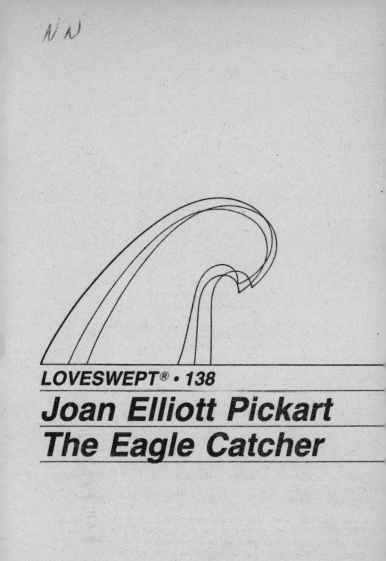

LOVESWEPT® • 138

Joan Elliott Pickart
The Eagle Catcher

BANTAM BOOKS
TORONTO · NEW YORK · LONDON · SYDNEY · AUCKLAND

THE EAGLE CATCHER

A Bantam Book / April 1986

*LOVESWEPT® and the wave device are registered
trademarks of Bantam Books, Inc. Registered in U.S. Patent
and Trademark Office and elsewhere.*

ISBN 0-553-21757-7

Published simultaneously in the United States and Canada

*Bantam Books are published by Bantam Books, Inc. Its
trademark, consisting of the words "Bantam Books" and
the portrayal of a rooster, is Registered in U.S. Patent and
Trademark Office and in other countries. Marca Registrada.
Bantam Books, Inc., 666 Fifth Avenue, New York, New
York 10103.*

PRINTED IN THE UNITED STATES OF AMERICA

O   0 9 8 7 6 5 4 3 2 1

With special thanks to the personnel at Davis-Monthan Air Force Base, Edwards Air Force Base, and Williams Air Force Base for their assistance and enthusiasm.

One

The city began to come alive after the long, dark night. The sun crept from behind the mountains, tentatively at first, sending streaking fingers of purple, orange, and yellow across the sky. Then the golden globe emerged and chased the last of the shadows into oblivion.

To some, the new day would bring hours of relaxing by a pool, an invigorating golf game, shopping trips to the multitude of stores. To the "snowbirds" who had escaped the cruel winter of the east and north, Phoenix, Arizona, was a haven from the storm, an oasis of pleasure in the desert.

But for the majority of people in the city, it was business as usual; jobs to hurry to, children to tend, lives to lead, just as they had the day before.

January, to the permanent residents of Phoenix, was the heart of their winter, when the sun was not as warm, the sky not as blue, and when heavier clothes were pulled from closets in direct contrast to the vacationers' flimsy attire.

Heather Wade turned off the shrill alarm and groaned, burrowing beneath the blankets on her bed. She lay still, but as sleep began to drift over her again, she threw back the covers and padded into the bathroom in her red flannel granny gown. Twenty minutes later she emerged, freshly showered, then dressed in brown corduroy slacks and a matching jacket, a cream-colored blouse with a soft bow at the neck, and stylish leather boots.

She brushed the short, dark curls that floated around her face, then applied mascara to the lashes framing her large dark eyes. A quick stroke of a light blusher on each cheek, rose-colored lipstick, and she was ready, with one thought in mind. Coffee.

A few minutes later she sank onto a chair at the table in the middle of her cheerful yellow kitchen, a mug of the desired brew in her hand.

"Wake up, Heather," she mumbled, plopping her elbow on the table and resting her chin in her hand. She hated mornings, she thought. Always had, always would. Mornings were insulting, a rude jolt to a person's nervous system. One should be allowed to wake slowly, leisurely, not be screamed at by a clock announcing the end of the delicious cocoon of sleep. Mornings were definitely grim. She drained her mug. "Go to work, Heather," she said, then pushed herself to her feet, snatched up her purse, and left the apartment.

She bypassed the elevator and walked down the four flights of outside stairs leading to the parking lot at the back of the building. Mentally sifting through what would require her immediate attention when she arrived at the travel agency, she rummaged through her purse for the keys to her compact car. When she reached the bottom of the stairs she looked up, then came to a complete halt and gasped in surprise. Taking up her entire line of vision was an enormous moving van that was blocking access to her car.

"Well, for Pete's sake," she said. "This is cute. Hello? Is anybody home? Hey! Somebody move this thing!"

A tall figure appeared from around the end of the van and walked slowly toward her. The man was dressed in faded jeans and a long-sleeved black flannel shirt. Heather's gaze flickered over wide shoulders that stretched the material of the shirt to capacity, long muscular legs that strained against the jeans, and then moved up to the man's face as he stopped in front of her.

"You rang?" he said, his voice deep and rich, his white teeth flashing as he smiled at her.

Good heavens, she thought, what a gorgeous man! What gorgeous thick black hair, what a gorgeous, ruggedly handsome face. And that body! *This* was one *gorgeous* hunk of stuff!

"Ma'am?" he said.

"What? Oh. Yes, well, could you move your truck? You're blocking my car and I have to get to work."

"Oh, I see. Well, I'd like to oblige, but I don't have the keys."

"You lost the keys?"

"No, I never had them." He smiled at her engagingly, then shoved his hands into his back pockets, causing his shirt to pull even tighter across his broad chest.

Just gorgeous! Heather thought wildly.

"Sorry," he said, lifting one shoulder in a shrug, "but I can't help you."

"Now, wait a minute. Who has the keys?"

"The driver. He went for coffee. I'm waiting for him and the other guy to get back."

"Wonderful," she muttered. "Didn't you people realize you were blocking the parking lot when you pulled in here?"

"Guess not. You're in a rush, huh?"

"I certainly am! I have a job to get to. I can't stand around while you muscle boys have breakfast!"

"Muscle boys?" He chuckled, and the rumbling sound feathered a funny sensation up Heather's spine. "I've never been called a muscle boy before. Have I been insulted?"

"Well, no, of course not. I mean, anyone who totes heavy furniture for a living needs a good physique to—That is—Oh, forget it!" she finished as a flush of embarrassment warmed her cheeks.

The man put his head back and roared with

laughter. "You're blushing!" he said, merriment dancing in his blue eyes.

"I am not!"

"Hey, I don't mind that you checked me over. It only makes us even, because I'm well aware of your lovely figure. Oh, yes, ma'am, very well aware."

Heather blinked once and swallowed heavily. The man's voice had seemed to drop an octave and had stroked her like dark velvet. His eyes were locked onto her's, and she felt pinned in place, unable to move nor hardly breathe.

"And then there are your eyes," he went on. "Great big, brown eyes, like a fawn's."

"Enough," she said sharply, snapping herself out of her trance. "It's a little early in the morning for a fast hustle, Mr. . . ."

"Dalton. Jace Dalton. I wasn't trying to hustle you. I meant every word as a sincere compliment."

"Spare me, okay? Just move that truck!"

"No keys, remember?" he said, still grinning. "I told you my name, and since we're keeping things even here, you should tell me yours."

"Wade. *Mrs.* Heather Wade."

"That's a lot of emphasis on the 'Mrs.' for someone who isn't wearing a wedding ring. Been divorced long?"

"No! I mean, yes! I mean . . . Mr. Dalton, you are a very rude, pushy man!"

"It's Jace, and I'm merely being observant. There's no Mr. Wade, right?"

"That's none of your business! Where's the joker who has the keys to this monstrosity?"

"I told you, they went for coffee."

"That's very irresponsible, you know. A person just doesn't plunk a huge moving van in the middle of a parking lot with no regard for those he might be inconveniencing."

"I thoroughly agree," Jace said solemnly, though Heather could detect a flicker of amusement in his eyes.

"I'll tell you this, Mr. Dalton. If I end up taking a taxi to work, I have every intention of submitting a bill for the fare to your moving company."

"That sounds very reasonable. Is your boss going to be all upset if you're late?"

"I don't have a boss, I have a partner, and we count on each other to be prompt."

"You have your own business? I'm impressed," Jace said. "You're very young to be half owner of . . . whatever."

"A travel agency, Mr. Dalton. Look, couldn't you track down the man with the keys?"

"I don't know where they went, and it's Jace. What's the name of your agency?"

"Wishing Well Travel. Why? Planning a trip? I'd think you get enough roaming around hauling furniture across the country. Not that I'd discourage a prospective client, of course. Where do you think you'd like to go?"

"To bed."

Her eyes widened. "I beg your pardon?"

"I've been driving half the night, and I'd like to get this van unloaded and get to bed. I'm really beat."

"Oh. Good idea," Heather said brightly. "Let's go find the guy with the keys and get this show on the road."

"*I* could drive you to work," Jace said.

"Sure you could. We'll hot-wire that van and zoom off. If we could move it at all, I could get to my car and—"

"I have my own car. I didn't ride in the van. The least I can do is see that you get to work on time. What do you say, Heather?"

Not smart, she thought, looking up at Jace Dalton. A person didn't go trundling off in a car with a total stranger. Good grief but he was good looking! She guessed he was thirty-seven or -eight, and he had a smattering of gray near his temples. The crinkly laugh lines by his eyes added character and—No. She was definitely not going anywhere with this epitome of masculinity. He'd already done tricky little things to her equilibrium with his sexy chuckles and intense gazes.

"Well?" he asked.

"No. No, thank you," she said. "It was kind of you to offer, but I can't accept."

"Would your husband object?"

"I don't have a—Very clever, Mr. Dalton. You have now firmly established that there is no Mr. Wade."

"It's Jace, Heather."

"Yes, well . . . Jace, I think I'll just go back up to my apartment and call for a taxi."

"Won't be necessary. Here comes the muscle boys."

"Good heavens, they're huge!"

"I'll just stand here and keep my mouth shut while you give 'em hell," Jace said.

"Thanks a bunch."

"Hey, buddy," one of the burly men said as the pair approached, "whata you say we get this stuff upstairs?"

"Excuse me," Heather said, "but you gentlemen are blocking my car with your truck. So, if it wouldn't be too much trouble, could you just move the van a teeny-tiny bit so I can squeeze my little-bitty car out of there?"

"You bet, ma'am," one of the men said. "Sorry for the trouble."

"That's perfectly all right," she said, refusing to look at a grinning Jace.

A minute later the huge van roared into action and moved farther down the parking lot, leaving Heather ample room to get to her car. She hurried to the car and unlocked it, only to have Jace reach around her and open the door for her.

"Ma'am," he said, smiling broadly as she slid behind the wheel. Instead of closing the door, he crossed his arms over the top of it. "Have a nice day, Heather Wade," he said quietly. "I'm very glad I met you. I'm looking forward to seeing you again."

"That's not very likely, Mr. . . . Jace. I'm sure you'll be on the road in a few hours."

"You own a travel agency so you know what a small world it is. We'll see each other again. You can count on it."

"May I have my door?" she asked, frowning. "I'm running terribly late."

"You bet," he said, and closed the door.

Heather quickly turned the key in the ignition, backed up, then drove out of the parking lot. As she glanced at the rearview mirror she saw Jace Dalton staring after her, his arms crossed over his chest.

Gorgeous, she thought, letting out a deep breath before inching into the traffic. Just sinfully gorgeous.

Heather Wade, Jace thought. Pretty little thing, with her big brown eyes and bouncy curls. She was tiny, like a china doll, and made a man very aware of his own strength. Mr. Wade was a fool for losing a sweet package like Heather. Jace would see Heather again, all right, and a lot sooner than she expected.

"Hey, buddy, you ready?" the driver called. "We'll haul it, you tell us where you want it put. Apartment four-twelve, right?"

"Yeah, that's the one," Jace said. "My new home."

Heather drove through the heavy traffic, frowning each time a red light caused her further delay. Her thoughts skittered back and forth between how late she was and Jace Dalton.

It hardly seemed fair, she decided, that one man should have been dished out so much of everything. Looks, build, charisma, blatant sexuality—

Jace had it all. He shouldn't be a furniture mover. He could be a model, a movie star, a centerfold, for Pete's sake. It had been a long time since a man had flustered her, since eyes had held her immobile, since a voice had seemed to stroke her like a velvet glove, causing a tingling sensation in the pit of her stomach. A very long time, indeed.

"Big macho deal," Heather said with an unladylike snort. Then she suddenly remembered that he had said she had eyes like a fawn. And a lovely figure. Did she really? "Oh, what a bunch of blarney!" she said. "Jace Dalton is a smooth-talking hustler. Thank goodness I'll never see *him* again! Oh, what a rotten shame. I'll never see him again!"

Laughing at her own foolishness, Heather parked behind the Wishing Well Travel office. Their agency was located in a small complex that housed a dozen different stores. She unlocked the back door and entered the small back room.

"Lori?" she called.

"Hi," her friend answered back. "I was just starting to get worried about you. Coffee's hot."

"I'm sorry I'm late," Heather said as she walked into the attractive front office. "I was held captive by a moving van." And, she added silently, a pirate in a black shirt, with hair as dark as the devil's own, and eyes as blue as . . . "Everything okay here?"

"Yep. Mrs. Pierson called again. Now she thinks they'll fly to Disneyland instead of driving. I said you'd figure the cost of air fare and add it to her land package."

"She's changed her mind three times already," Heather said. "I've done it with the bus and train fares. Oh, well, I'll start over and check the airlines this time."

"What did you say about a moving van?"

"It was parked in front of my car at the apartment and . . . Never mind, it's not a very interesting story except for the mover, who was the most beautiful man I've seen in my entire life."

"Really?" Lori said. "Did you talk to him?"

"Talk? My dear, we made mad, passionate love in the cab of the truck. It was awesome."

"Oh, go away," Lori said. "I'd stand on my chair and cheer if I thought it was true, but I know better. You *need* a sexy man in your life. A torrid affair would be perfect."

"So you've told me a hundred times," Heather said with a laugh. "I will repeat my standard answer. Thanks, but no thanks. Men are yummy creatures, but I don't want one."

"Fool that you are."

"I have a very pleasant social life."

"Pleasant is boring. The men you date come under the heading of 'good friends.' Yuck. Personally, I think you should go for the max and get married again. I adore being married. I can have sex anytime I want to, and Jerry still respects me in the morning. So, which do you want? An affair or marriage?"

"None of the above."

"Oh, you're such a dud, Heather."

" 'Tis true," she said cheerfully. "Well, I've got to get to work."

Lori muttered something under her breath as Heather settled into the chair behind her desk and flicked on the computer. Instead of checking the airline schedules for the Piersons' trip to Disneyland, though, Heather thought about her partner.

Lori Sanders was the total opposite in appearance of Heather. Lori was tall, five-foot-ten, and had blond hair and sparkling blue eyes. She had been married for seven years to Jerry Sanders, an accountant, and the only dark shadow in their union was their inability to have a child. Both had undergone endless tests, and there was no medical explanation as to why Lori had not conceived.

Heather and Lori had been best friends during their high school days in Phoenix, and then had kept in constant touch as their lives took them to opposite ends of the country. When Heather had returned to Phoenix three years before, the two had pooled their resources and started Wishing Well Travel after completing the necessary training course. The business was growing steadily, showing an increasing profit, and the women were pleased with their success.

Their ongoing banter concerning Heather's disinterest in a serious relationship with a man was conducted good-naturedly, although Lori was quite serious and Heather knew it. There had been no man of importance in her life since her husband, Russell. Lori wanted Heather to find a new love, but Heather adamantly stated time and again that she wasn't interested.

The day passed quickly. Heather telephoned Mrs. Pierson with the airline information and Mrs. Pierson said she'd think it over. Heather rolled her eyes. Heather and Lori then arranged a bus tour to Nogales, Sonora, Mexico, for a group of winter visitors. Lori was to accompany the tourists, and she was looking forward to the daylong excursion.

At six o'clock they closed the office and bid each other good night, Heather vowing to be on time in the morning.

"Hey," Lori said, "if you get a chance to make love in the truck again, go for it. For that, you should take the whole day off."

"I'll keep it in mind," Heather said. " 'Night. Tell jazzy Jerry hello for me."

"I will. Say, there's a new guy in Jerry's office who—"

"No!"

"Pooh!"

Heather drove at a crawl in the rush-hour traffic and was more than ready to turn into the parking lot behind her apartment building. As she pulled into her parking place and turned off the ignition, she once again thought of Jace Dalton. There was no sign of the moving van, and she surmised that Jace was halfway to Timbuktu by now.

"He deserted me," she said dramatically as she got out of the car. "Me! The lovely creature with eyes like a fawn's. Is there no justice?"

She strolled around to the front of the building

to check her mailbox in the lobby, then rode up to the fourth floor in the elevator. She absently glanced through her mail as she walked down the carpeted hallway to her apartment. The sound of a blaring stereo grew louder and louder as she neared her door, and she halted in front of the apartment next to hers.

"New neighbor in four-twelve," she muttered. "A loud new neighbor. Wonderful. Oh, why did quiet Mrs. Greenberg go to live with her daughter?"

Entering her own apartment, Heather tossed her purse and mail on the lemon-yellow sofa and planted her hands on her hips as she stared at the wall.

Polite, but firm, she thought. That was the best course of action. She'd march over there and get this noise level nonsense straightened out. She definitely had the right to peace and quiet in her own home. With a determined tilt to her chin, she strode down the hall to apartment 412. She knocked briskly on the door, then gasped in surprise as the door swung open.

"Hello?" she called, peering in.

The living room was strewn with boxes, some half empty, their contents scattered on the floor. Large brown and tan furniture had been set in place, and the stereo, from which the rock music was blasting, was part of a home-entertainment center against the far wall.

"Anyone home?" she shouted over the din. "Hello? Oh, the heck with this." She stomped across the room and snapped off the stereo. "Is there anyone—Oh!"

She turned, and her eyes widened when she saw the figure sprawled on the sofa, sound asleep.

"Jace!" she said. "Oh, good heavens, it's Jace!"

She walked closer, peering down at the sleeping man. One arm was across his chest, while his other arm was hanging to the floor. Long lashes fanned against his lean cheeks, and a slight shadow of beard was just beginning to show on his face. A lock of his thick, dark hair had tumbled boyishly onto his forehead, and Heather resisted the urge to brush it back into place.

"Gorgeous," she whispered. He was so big and strong. Even asleep he had an aura of power about him. But what was he doing here? she wondered. Of course! He'd said he was terribly tired. He must have fallen asleep after they'd finished moving the new tenants' belongings in. He was trespassing, could end up in jail if the people living there showed up. Falling asleep in other folks' houses was fine for Goldilocks, but . . . "Jace" she said, placing her fingertip on his forehead. "Jace, wake up."

"Mmm."

"Jace, come on. You've got to get out of here."

"Mmm."

"Jace Dalton," she yelled, "move your tush!"

"What!" He sat bolt upright and nearly toppled off the sofa.

"Are you awake?" Heather asked.

"Huh? Heather? Is that you?" He blinked his eyes several times.

"Jace, you can't sleep here. You've got to leave."

"Why?" he asked, swinging his feet to the floor and looking up at her. "Is the building on fire?"

"No. Listen, if the people who live here show up and find you, they're liable to throw a fit. Moving men aren't supposed to sack out in the customers' living room."

"Moving . . . Oh, yeah, right," he said, a smile tugging at the corners of his mouth. "That's not socially acceptable, is it?"

"Not hardly."

"How did you get in here?"

"The door was open. The stereo was blasting right through my wall, and I came over to ask the new tenant to turn it down."

"You live next door?"

"Yes, in four-fourteen."

"I'll be damned." He grinned. "See? I told you it was a small world."

"Jail cells are smaller. You've got to get out of here, Jace."

He stretched his long arms across the top of the sofa and smiled at her.

"You wouldn't want me to end up in jail?" he asked.

"No, of course not."

"That's really nice of you, Heather. Really, really nice. How was your day at the travel agency?"

"Oh, fine. We—Jace, aren't you listening to me? You can't be found in here."

"Well, you're here too. Maybe they'll put us both in the same cell in the clink."

"That's not funny! Come on."

"Where are we going?"

"Out of this apartment. The tenants could show up any minute. Let's go!"

"Yes, ma'am," he said, pushing himself to his feet. "I'm right behind you."

Jace turned off the light and stepped out into the hall with Heather, pulling the door closed behind him.

"I'm hungry," he said. "How about going out for something to eat?"

"Well, I . . ."

"Have you had dinner?"

"No, but . . ."

"Great. Where would you like to go? It will be my way of thanking you for keeping me out of the clutches of the law."

"I can't go out to dinner with you."

"Why not?"

"I really don't know you, Jace. I'm not in the habit of going out with strangers."

"Oh. Well, we'll stay in then."

" 'In'?"

"At your place. We can have some eggs or something, chat a little, whatever it takes to change my status from stranger to someone you know. Actually, you do know me. I'm the man who said you have eyes like a fawn's and a lovely figure."

"Don't start *that* again," Heather said, frowning

as she felt the now familiar tingling up her spine. "All right, I'll make us an omelet."

"You're most kind."

"This is absurd," she said, spinning around and heading down the hall. "I won't go out with you because I don't know you, so I invite you into my apartment. Ludicrous."

Jace chuckled softly and Heather groaned silently. That sexy sound. She really wished he wouldn't do that!

"Say," Jace said when they entered her living room, "this is nice. That place next door is a mess. I really like what you've done in here. It's bright and cheerful. Looks like you."

"Thank you. Why don't you sit down while I change my clothes, and then I'll fix us some dinner."

Jace watched as Heather went into the bedroom and shut the door. Pretty, pretty lady, he thought. She'd been cute as a button when she'd stood there all in a flutter because he, the moving man, was going to get tossed in the slammer for crashing on the customer's sofa. So, now what? It had been fun while it lasted, but enough was enough. He'd better tell her that *he* was her new neighbor with the loud stereo. He sure hoped she thought it was hilarious, because he didn't want her to get all in a huff. After all, they were neighbors and should be friendly.

Friendly? he thought. He'd like to be more than just a friend to Heather Wade. Her eyes were enough to turn a man inside out. Everything about her was so damn feminine and appealing. But she was cautious, wary, and he'd better watch his step. First thing he had to do was tell her the truth about who he was. If she thought he was going to climb into his eighteen-wheeler and disappear into the sunset, she was very, very wrong. He was there to stay, right next door.

Heather changed into jeans and a red sweater, then flicked a brush through her hair to create a halo of soft curls around her head. Jace Dalton, she thought, was sitting in her living room! Sexy Jace, in all his magnificent male splendor was on the other side of that door! And she was totally out of her mind for allowing him to be there! She didn't even know him. She had never in her life done anything so stupid. Of course, the affect that Jace had on her nervous system wasn't exactly normal either. She'd just stuff him full of omelet and bid him adieu.

"Dinnertime," she sang out as she hurried through the living room to the kitchen.

"Want some help?" Jace asked, following her and leaning against the kitchen doorjamb.

"What? Oh, no, no, you just go relax. How many eggs do you like in your omelet?"

"Six."

"Six?" she repeated, turning to look at him. "Six eggs?"

"Or whatever. I don't want to use up your whole supply."

"I have plenty, but that will make a huge omelet. But, then, you're a huge man, so I guess that makes sense. Big man, big appetite for . . . stuff. I'm babbling."

He smiled. "You certainly are. Do I make you nervous?"

"Well, not you per se, you understand. It's just the circumstances under which you came to be here. I sort of snarfed you up and dragged you in. I usually don't do things like this."

"Look, maybe it would help if I told you that I'm—"

"Harmless? Ha! I'll bet you haven't been harmless since the day you were born. Oh, I'm being silly. I'm twenty-seven-years old and acting like a child. Ignore me."

"That's a tough assignment, Heather Wade," he said, pushing himself away from the doorjamb and walking slowly toward her.

"What is?" she asked, her heart starting to do a tap dance.

"Ignoring you. In fact, it's totally impossible. I'd be more inclined to kiss you than ignore you."

She stared up at him. "You would?"

"I would," he said, cupping her face in his hands and lowering his head. "I certainly would."

He brushed his lips over hers, and an involuntary hum of pleasure escaped from her throat. His tongue slid along her bottom lip, then invaded her mouth as he dropped his arms to enfold her, to crush her breasts against the hard wall of his chest. She encircled his neck with her hands and inched her fingers into his night-dark hair. Their tongues met and dueled, and Heather leaned heavily against his solid body. Passions soared. Heartbeats quickened. Breathing became labored and raspy in the quiet room as the kiss went on and on.

Heather seemed to float away from herself, saw herself from afar in hazy, detached fascination. She was being kissed by Jace Dalton, and was returning the kiss with total abandon. Long-forgotten desires deep within her sparked a wondrous trembling throughout her body.

Jace's hands slid down over the slope of her buttocks to pull her closer yet, to fit her tightly to him. His manhood pressed against her, heated, strong, announcing his want and need of her. Heather heard a soft moan, but didn't know if it had come from her throat or his. It didn't matter. Nothing mattered.

"Heather," Jace murmured, his voice gritty with desire. "Oh, Heather."

"Hmmm?" she said dreamily, slowly lifting her lashes. "Oh!" she gasped, snapping back to reality and wiggling out of his arms. "Oh, dear me!"

"What's wrong?" he asked, taking a shuddering breath.

"I can't believe this!" she said, shaking her head. "I don't kiss men I don't know! In fact, I don't even kiss men I *know* the way I just—I really can't believe I did that!"

He smiled. "Did you hate it?"

"Well, no. But that's beside the point!"

"Not, it's not. We shared a fantastic kiss that we both enjoyed, and I think that's great."

"But I don't even know you!"

"You really have a thing about that, don't you? Well, I'm going to put your mind at ease. Heather Wade, I would like to officially introduce myself. Madam, I, Jace Dalton, am your new neighbor!"

Two

"I beg your pardon?" Heather asked, her voice hardly above a whisper. "You're my what?"

"Your neighbor," Jace said. "I'm four-twelve, the loud stereo. Heather, your mouth is open."

"Oh," she said, snapping it closed.

"So, you see, you and I—"

"Now, hold it just a minute here, bub!" she yelled. "What kind of game are you playing? You're a muscle boy, a mover, a . . . Aren't you?"

"Nope."

"You said you were."

"No, *you* said I was."

"I did? I did not! If you're my neighbor, why did you let me drag you out of your own apartment?"

He shrugged. "It seemed like a good idea at the time. I was really glad to see you, and when you adamantly stated we should haul it out of there, I just hauled. Now, let's eat. I'm starving."

"No!"

"Hey, you're not angry about this, are you? I didn't lie, you know. You assumed some things and I simply didn't correct you. That's a long way from lying."

"You sound like a politician," she said, frowning. "Sneaky. You know what I mean?"

"Well, I do work for the government, but I—"

"A-ha! I knew it! A politician."

He laughed. "No, I'm not. Aren't you going to feel guilty if I pass out from hunger?"

"Not very," she said, opening the refrigerator and taking out an egg carton. "Can you make toast?"

"Sure. How tough can it be? Where's the bread?"

"You're really my neighbor?"

"Yep. I'll come over tomorrow and borrow a cup of sugar. That'll convince you. I might borrow a cup of coffee too. I don't have any food at my place. Not that it matters. I can't cook worth a damn."

"Oh?" Heather said, cracking eggs in a bowl. "You've always had someone to cook for you?"

"I eat at the—Oh, you mean a wife? No, I've never been married."

"Why not?"

"Marriage just didn't fit into my scheme of things, I guess. How long were you married?"

"Two years," she said, pouring the eggs into a frying pan.

"And how long has it been since Mr. Wade's been around?"

"Three years. Are you making toast?"

"Oh, yeah, sure." He stuck the bread in the toaster and pushed down the lever. "You're a beautiful woman, Heather. I'm surprised you haven't remarried by now."

"I'm not interested in marrying again."

"I see." He nodded. "It was a nasty divorce, huh? Look, I'm not trying to be nosy. I'd just like to get to know you better, understand who you are, where you're coming from. If you don't want to talk about your divorce, it's fine with me."

"I'm not divorced, Jace," she said quietly, not looking at him. "I'm a widow. My husband, Russ, was killed a week before our two-year anniversary."

"Damn. I'm sorry, Heather. I just assumed . . . I'm really sorry."

"That's all right," she said, smiling at him. "It was a long time ago. I've glued myself back together and have a new life. The toast is done. The butter is on the counter there. Dinner is served, Mr. Dalton. Let it not be said that Heather Wade would let a muscle boy go hungry."

"I'm your neighbor!"

"But how do I know that?"

"I'll let you help me unpack and put everything away."

"I'd love to. I enjoy making order out of chaos. I doubt if you'd want me rummaging around in your belongings, though."

"Are you serious? I'd be eternally grateful for the

slightest clue as to where to begin. I've got a real disaster over there. But you worked hard all day. I can't ask you to take that on."

"It'll be fun," Heather said, setting their plates on the table. "Ready to eat?"

"Very," he said, sitting down. "Looks great." A widow, he thought. Damn, he'd sure put his foot in his mouth. He'd just naturally assumed she was divorced. She'd had it rough. She'd been so damn young to face all of that.

"Now then," Heather said, "you have a choice. You can have your coffee in a Dallas Cowboys mug, or in a Green Bay Packers one. Take your pick."

"No contest. Give me Green Bay."

"And what, pray tell, do you have against Dallas?" she asked, sitting down opposite him.

They immediately launched into an animated discussion regarding the attributes of the football teams in question, and were still at it as they loaded the dishwasher.

"And furthermore—" Jace said.

"Enough," Heather interrupted, laughing. "You obviously don't know diddly about football. Come on. Let's go see if we can find your living room floor."

"Even if the entire crummy Dallas Cowboys team showed up to help, my place would still be a wreck."

"Have you no faith?"

"Mmm," he said dubiously.

In Jace's living room, Heather peered into a box, nodded in approval, then loaded Jace's arms with towels and sheets. He mumbled something under his breath as she pointed him in the direction of the linen closet, and she decided she was better off not knowing what he had said.

She sat Indian style on the floor and pulled another box in front of her. Inside was a conglomeration of memorabilia, which, she decided, in Jace's case was a polite word for junk. She placed on the carpet a gnarled piece of driftwood, a nondescript rock, and a pencil holder fashioned out of a beer can. Her hand stopped in midair when she saw the next object, and she reached for it tentatively.

It was a model of an Air Force jet, about eight inches in length and painted a shiny silver. She cradled it in both hands and stared at it, her heart racing.

"Okay," Jace said, coming back into the room. "I crammed all that into the cupboard. Now what should I—Heather? What's wrong? You're white as a ghost."

"What?" she asked, looking up at him as if surprised to see him there.

"Hey, something upset you," he said, squatting down beside her. "Does it have to do with that model?"

"I'm sorry," she said, setting it on the floor. "It just brought back a lot of memories."

"Of what?"

"Oh, Jace, you don't want to hear my tale of woe."

"Humor me," he said, smiling at her.

"Well, you see," she said, sighing deeply, "my husband was a Buff pilot. A Buff is a B-52. I met him while he was stationed here at Williams in the Air Force. After we were married he was transferred to Langley. He was in charge of training new crews, and he was gone continually, it seemed. Then one night they were flying in a storm and Russ tried to land, and . . . and they crashed. Everyone on board was killed."

Jace stiffened, every muscle in his body becoming tightly coiled as he clenched his jaw. Dammit, he thought, an Air Force pilot!

"Jace?"

"What? Oh, I was just thinking that you'd been dealt a lousy hand."

"I knew what I was getting into when I married Russ. Well, at least I thought I did. I think I pretended the danger wasn't there, that they'd miraculously change the training schedules so he'd come home every night for dinner like other men. The Air Force was his life and I got the leftovers."

"You weren't happy?" Jace asked gently.

"It was . . . stressful. Russ was away more than he was home. I lived for the times he would be there and felt empty when he left. When he died it was as though I didn't know who I was anymore. I lost me, myself, while I was married. I loved Russ, but I could never do that again, lose myself because I loved someone."

"I don't think love and marriage is supposed to be like that, Heather. I'm no expert on the subject, but . . . No, I don't think so." Not that he'd even been in love, he thought, but he knew plenty of people who were. She had it all wrong. What difference did it make anyway? he asked himself. He wasn't interested in love and marriage either. But still . . . "Heather," he said, "this thing about losing yourself when you love. The people I know don't—"

"Wait. I didn't say it right, I guess. I was referring only to myself. I know there are wonderful marriages. It's me, personally, who didn't do it correctly. I loved Russ so deeply that I was nothing unless he was with me. That's not very healthy. Then when he died . . . Well, I just never intend to love again."

"But you're older now, more mature. You see the error you made, and you'd retain your identity next time around. Damn, Heather, you've sentenced yourself to a lifetime of loneliness over something that happened when you were a young girl."

"I'm not lonely. You're not married. Are you lonely?"

"I don't think so."

"See? Different strokes for different folks. Love is not my cup of tea."

"I see," Jace said quietly.

"So, enough about me," she said, forcing a smile. "Tell me about Jace Dalton, former muscle boy. What do you do for the government? Heavens, you're not with the Internal Revenue, are you?"

"No, I'm not a taxman. I'm a . . . technical adviser . . . of sorts."

"What do you give technical advice about?"

"High-tech stuff. Classified."

"Oh, you can't talk about it?"

"Not right now," he said, a frown knitting his dark brows together.

"How exciting! Just like on television. Where did you move from?"

"Michigan."

"Then you must be enjoying our mild weather."

"I haven't been out in it much yet, but I'm sure I will. Look, I hope you're not still upset because you talked about your husband. I shouldn't have pushed you about it, I guess, but I meant it when I said I want to know you better, understand who you are."

Heather ran her fingertip over the smooth surface of the model airplane, then turned to look at Jace, smiling warmly.

"I'm not upset," she said. "You're very easy to talk to. It was nice of you to listen."

Their gazes met, held, and an almost eerie silence fell over the room. Eons of seconds passed, and neither moved. Then Jace slowly lifted his hand and cradled it against her cheek, his thumb stroking the soft skin.

"I want to kiss you, Heather," he said, his voice slightly husky, "but I'm not going to. I don't want to do anything to make you angry, or to frighten you. I suppose I should apologize for kissing you before, but I'm really not sorry, because it was fantastic."

But she wanted him to kiss her! Heather thought. What was wrong with her? Jace touched her, and she melted. Jace kissed her, and she didn't want the kiss to end. Jace held her in his strong arms, and she felt safe, as though having found a haven. Why? Why was he capable of making her so aware of her own femininity, of filling her with desire? What was it about this man, this Jace Dalton? She had shared so many of her inner thoughts and secrets with him as naturally as breathing. And her body? Heavens, her body was going crazy! Jace was very, very dangerous.

"Okay, boss," he said, breaking the crackling tension between them, "what's my next assignment?" He pushed himself to his feet in a smooth, powerful motion. "Towels are boring."

"Try glasses in kitchen cupboards," Heather said, willing her heart to stop its erratic beat. "They're a peak experience."

"Mmm."

They worked steadily for the next two hours. Heather offered to help Jace put his clothes away, but he refused. He also snatched one box from her as she was about to open it, saying it was full of silly, personal things, and he hid it in the bedroom closet. She wondered what sort of silly, personal things he didn't want her to see, but figured it was wiser not to ask. Finally, Jace said that his conscience was bothering him, and Heather was not to put away another thing.

"I think I found some new muscles," she said as she stretched. "But we made very good progress."

"And I thank you, I really do. As soon as I find the blankets for the bed, I've got it made."

"Excellent. Well, good night, Jace," she said, and started toward the door.

He caught up with her in two long strides and lightly gripped her shoulders. Damn, he wanted to kiss her, he thought. He really needed to kiss this woman!

" 'Night, Jace," she said softly, not turning around.

"Yeah," he said, dropping his hands and stepping back. "Thanks again."

After Heather had closed the door behind her, Jace drew a steadying breath, then went in search of the blankets. He rummaged through a box and found them, along with a pillow, and made up the bed. His gaze shifted to the closet, and he walked across the room and opened the double doors. Reaching in, he pulled out a hanger and held it at arm's length, staring at the garment.

"You're in trouble, Jace," he said. "It's blue, but it might as well be a red flag in front of a bull. When Heather finds out . . . Damn."

His gaze swept over the Air Force uniform he held, the silver wings above the breast pocket, the four rows of ribbons, his nameplate, the silver eagles with spread wings on the shoulders. With a frown, he replaced the jacket, then sank onto the edge of the bed.

Well, Colonel Dalton, he asked himself, now what? He'd met a woman who stirred something within him. Not just physical desire, but something new, different, a feeling of protectiveness. But he had lost his chance to discover more about

Heather before he had even had an opportunity to begin! She was dead set against any kind of involvement, and then to top it off, her husband had been a Buff pilot who'd died in a plane crash. He'd skittered around telling Heather he was in the Air Force. He was a test pilot, for cripe's sake, which to Heather would be as popular as the plague.

He should be glad she wasn't husband-hunting, he told himself. They'd have a good time, then . . . No, he didn't believe that for a minute. He'd never play games with Heather. She deserved better than that. She was special, and she should be cherished, cared for. Definitely out of the ordinary sentiments for him, but they were creeping in on him, all right. What was it about her? Why was she getting to him like this? Well, one thing was for damn sure. He wasn't being tossed out of the ball game before he'd had his turn at bat. He'd give her time, move slowly, then tell her about his career at the right moment.

Heather Wade hadn't seen the last of him, not by a long shot. He'd be damned if he'd let her past rob them of today, and what they might share in the future. The future? He shook his head. He didn't dwell on the future, never had. He lived one day at a time. Then why was he suddenly thinking about tomorrow and the possibility of seeing, holding, kissing Heather Wade?

"Go unpack a box, colonel," he growled, striding from the room. "You're working your brain overtime and turning it into oatmeal."

At two A.M. Jace glanced around and decided the apartment was in livable order. He'd tote the empty boxes to the trash tomorrow, get some food in, and everything would be ship-shape. He showered, then turned off the light and slid naked between the sheets on the bed. His thoughts immediately centered on Heather.

"Ah, hell," he said into the darkness, "not now. I'll toss and turn all night if I think about . . ." A shaft of heat shot across the lower regions of his body. "Dammit!"

At last Jace slept, only to be plagued by a strange, haunting dream. He was flying a silver jet. Another plane approached him, piloted by Heather. He chased her through the clouds as she laughed and beckoned him to follow her. But then she disappeared from view and he was left alone. Totally alone. He woke before dawn, his body glistening with sweat, and stared blindly up into the darkness.

When the alarm went off Heather rendered the clock a solid whack, then rolled over onto her back. And almost immediately the thought of Jace Dalton penetrated the foggy state of her mind.

How long had it been since she'd gone to sleep thinking of a man, then awakened in the morning just to think of him again? she wondered. And, oh, what a man was Jace Dalton. So big and strong, so incredibly handsome, so easy to talk to. Goodness, what a list she was creating. And she mustn't forget his kiss and touch and . . .

"Oh, my," she said, as desire shot through her and her breasts grew taut. "This will never do."

A short time later Heather was showered and dressed in blue slacks and a blue-and-white-striped sweater. Jace had no food in his apartment, she thought, as she waited for the coffee to drip. Should she take him a cup of coffee? No, that was rather forward. Besides, he might still be asleep. Well, she could knock on his door. He'd never hear her if he was sleeping, because he slept like a dead person. It would be a nice gesture on her part to take him a mug of coffee. Just a friendly, neighborly thing to do. Oh, what the heck, why not?

Jace had finished buttoning his shirt and was reaching for his tie when a knock sounded at the door. He walked into the living room, then hesitated as he touched the doorknob.

Heather? he wondered. No, probably not. But . . . "Yes?" he said.

"Jace? It's Heather. I brought you a cup of coffee."

"Oh. Great. Just . . . um . . . just a minute. I have to get my pants on." Think, Dalton! he commanded himself, glancing at his uniform. Dark slacks, light blue shirt, both custom-made. Maybe if he didn't put on the tie with the four-in-hand knot, he'd look like a civilian. There were no insignia on his shirt, nothing to indicate he was in the service. But, hell, he thought, Heather had been married to an Air Force man. She'd probably peg his clothes as a uniform in a second. But maybe not. Except for his belt. It was standard issue, webbed with a solid silver buckle. He had to get rid of the belt.

Jace strode back into the bedroom and pulled the belt from the loops of his pants. He opened two buttons on his shirt, then plastered what he hoped was a casual expression on his face as he returned to the living room and opened the door.

"Hi," he said. "This is really very nice of you. Come on in."

"Well, I for one cannot survive without my morning coffee, so I thought I'd bring you a cup." Heather handed him the mug, somehow managing to drag her gaze away from his magnificent body. She looked beyond him into the apartment. "Goodness, your place is neat as a pin. You must have been up half the night."

"Just about," he said, gesturing her in and shutting the door behind her.

"You look like you're ready to report in," she said.

"Report in?" he repeated, stiffening slightly.

"To your new job."

"Oh, yeah, right. That's where I'm going. Can you sit down for a minute?"

"Only that long. I have to get to work. I guess today is for the color blue," she said, sinking onto the plush sofa. "We look like the Bobbsey Twins."

"Yeah," he said, smiling weakly. So far, so good,

he thought. She didn't realize she was looking at an Air Force uniform. Now he just had to make sure she was safely away from the building before he popped out in his jacket. How had he gotten himself into this cloak and dagger stuff? "The coffee is great," he said. "You're leaving for work soon?"

"Right now," she said, glancing at her watch, then getting to her feet.

"Heather, will you have dinner with me tonight?" he asked. He set his mug on the coffee table and stood beside her.

"Well, yes, that sounds very nice," she said.

"Seven o'clock? If I'm going to be later than that, I'll call you. The first day on a new . . . job can get a little complicated."

"All right." She smiled and started for the door. "I'll see you tonight. Have a nice day."

"It's been pretty good for me so far," he said, closing the distance between them and holding out his hand. "I really would like to kiss you, Heather, but I said I wouldn't frighten you in any way."

Heather seemed powerless to stop herself as she placed her hand in Jace's and allowed him to pull her against him. He claimed her mouth in a long, searing kiss that sent shock waves of desire spiraling through her. She twined her arms about his neck and returned the kiss urgently, ignoring the voice in her head that screamed its disapproval. Being held and kissed by Jace Dalton felt so right, so good, and she savored each moment of ecstasy.

"Until tonight," he said, his voice strained when he finally released her.

"Yes," she said, hoping her legs would carry her to the door. " 'Bye."

"See ya."

What kissing that woman did to him was a sin! Jace thought after she had left. At least he'd bought himself a little time. He'd tell her tonight that he was an Air Force colonel and hoped she didn't dump him flat. He'd rather wait awhile, give her a chance to accept him as a man, but this sneaking around stuff was hard on the nerves!

He paced the floor for ten minutes, then finished dressing and left his apartment. The sunlight reflected off the silver eagles on his shoulders as he settled his brimmed field cap onto his head and walked down the four flights of stairs to the parking lot. He was relieved when he saw that Heather's car was gone.

As he started toward his car he met a woman in her fifties. "Oh, I do adore a man in uniform," she said. "You're a handsome devil, colonel. You're hard to resist in that spiffy blue uniform."

"I hope you're right," he said. "I know a lady who might be very unimpressed."

"Then she's a silly girl. Good day."

"Ma'am," he said. Unimpressed? he thought as he slid behind the wheel of his silver sports car. That was putting it mildly. Heather Wade was liable to tell him to take a long walk off a short pier!

*   *   *

"Okay, that's it," Lori said at one o'clock. "What's with you, Heather?"

"Huh?"

"You've sighed deeply at least a dozen times, and I've seen you stare off into space with a dopey expression on your face."

"Don't be silly," Heather said, busily shuffling papers on her desk.

"Spring fever in January? Nope. It's a man. It has to be a man. Who is he?"

"The moving van man. Well, he turned out to be my new neighbor, and I cooked him an omelet after I dragged him out of his apartment because I thought he'd go to jail for sleeping there. His name is Jace Dalton."

"Oh-h-h, what a sexy, macho name. This is wonderful, Heather. Wonderful! Did he kiss you?"

"Lori, this sounds like the conversations we had when we were fifteen years old."

"He kissed you," Lori said decisively. "Fantastic. When are you going to see him again?"

"Well, we're going out to dinner tonight—"

"This is too good to be true," Lori said, her eyes dancing with excitement. "I'm really happy for you, Heather."

"There's nothing to be happy about. I have a dinner date, that's all."

"Ha! You've been acting like a dewy-eyed kid all day. Jace darlin' has definitely had an affect on you."

"He's very nice," Heather said primly.

"And sexy as hell."

"And sexy as hell." Heather burst into laughter. "Is this the kind of stuff men talk about in locker rooms?"

"I think they're a little more descriptive."

"Oh. How gross. Lori?"

"Yes?"

"Jace is—different from anyone I've met before. He frightens me a little, because I don't think clearly when I'm around him and . . . I don't know, he just . . ."

"Oh, honey, don't be afraid of yourself or of Jace. You've shut off your feelings for so long, it's time for you to wake up and live again. Follow your heart, Heather. Promise me you will."

"We'll see," she said quietly.

At two o'clock Jace left the building housing the offices of the commanding officer of the base and his staff.

The briefing, he thought as he put his cap on, had not exactly been brief! Well, he'd known what his orders were before he arrived. The testing of the new X-82 jet was behind schedule. The prototype simulator and the jet were here at Williams, and he was to iron the kinks out and get that bird in the air. He definitely had his work cut out for him.

"Hey, if it isn't the Eagle Catcher!" a man yelled.

Jace looked at the man sprinting toward him. "Ed!" he said, a wide grin on his face.

"How in the hell are ya, colonel, suh?" Ed said, saluting sharply.

"Damn, it's good to see you, Ed," Jace said, extending his hand, which Ed shook vigorously.

"Darlin' boy, you are a sight for sore eyes," Ed said. "My butt is in the wringer over this project. I've tried every trick from here to Sunday, and that bird is a cold goose. So, I says to the brass, get the Eagle Catcher down here, 'cause, gentlemen, if he can't get it in the air, then it ainta gonna fly."

Jace laughed heartily and slapped Ed on the back as they strolled across the sprawling base. Ed Turner was shorter than Jace by several inches and had a boyish face topped by a shock of red hair. He was Southern born, and the degree of his accent depended on the mood he was in. They had flown together in Vietnam and had maintained their friendship in the years following.

"So, let's see this Tinkertoy of yours, major," Jace said.

"It's a beauty, Jace. Sleek as a woman's soft thigh. Damn thing won't get off the ground, though. Well, I was up a half dozen times in the simulator, but I crashed and burned. It's your baby now, darlin' boy, and I'm more than ready to take orders from you, 'cause I'm plum out of ideas."

"I'll do my best."

"Hey, when I checked at housing they said you were living off base. What's up?"

Jace shrugged. "I don't know. I got my orders and suddenly decided to take my stuff out of storage and get a place away from base."

"Uh-oh. Sounds like a man who's thinking about hanging up the blues. You due to re-up?"

"Yeah. My twenty years will be finished in six months."

"And?"

"I'll also be at the end of my test pilot rotation, Ed. Nobody gets an extension on their five years, you know that."

"You'd still be a pilot. I can't see you not flying, Jace. The Eagle Catcher was meant to be up there in the clouds."

"There are civilian flying jobs. Hell, I don't know. I'll make up my mind when the time comes, I guess."

"But living off base? That's a bit extreme. Oh, you've inherited my aide now that you're taking over. Flaky kid, but he's all right. I've been telling him all about the Eagle Catcher. The poor kid is shaking in his shorts. He thinks you breathe fire or something. We've got a good crew here, Jace. Top-notch civilians and blue-suiters. They're off today."

"So, let's take a look at this stubborn baby, Ace."

"Right this way, colonel, suh. Yes, suh, colonel, suh, it's all yours!"

The men showed their IDs to the two security officers stationed outside the hangar, then Ed pulled open the door and stepped back for Jace to enter. They strode across the echoing expanse. When they reached the X-82 Ed crossed his arms over his chest and smiled, watching as Jace walked slowly around the sleek silver jet.

"Sweet, sweet, sweet," Jace said. "Damn, this is a beautiful airplane."

"Didn't I tell you?"

"Well, the first order of business is to read the reports and computer printouts on what you've done so far. Let's go see this swanky office of mine."

"One thing for sure, Jace. Your stay in Phoenix won't be dull."

Jace looked up at the gleaming jet. Suddenly, the image of Heather Wade flashed before his eyes, and he smiled.

"Ed, old buddy," he said, "you're right about that. I think Phoenix will be very, very interesting. All the way around the block."

Three

The aide that Jace had inherited from Ed turned out to be a short, small-boned airman who was continually pushing his glasses up on his nose. Bruce Smith had saluted sharply when Jace and Ed entered the office, dropping a handful of papers in the process.

"Sorry, sirs," Bruce said, scrambling to retrieve the papers as he shoved his glasses into place.

"I need the computer printouts on the X-82, please," Jace said.

"Yes, sir. Oh, ouch!" Bruce exclaimed as he whacked his head on the desk.

Jace gave Ed a thanks-for-nothing look, and Ed laughed as they went into Jace's office. The two caught up on each other's lives as they drank cups of strong coffee, then Jace asked Ed for a verbal

44

report on the X-82. Ed was still talking when Bruce came in with his arms loaded with folders.

"The computer reports, sir," he said.

"Good," Jace said.

When Bruce didn't move Jace looked at him, then Ed, then back at the aide.

"Put them on the desk, airman," Jace said.

"Yes, sir." Bruce did as instructed. "Anything else, sir?"

"No, thank you."

"Very good, sir." Bruce saluted, then spun on his heel and left the room.

"Is he for real?" Jace asked, frowning.

"He's not so bad," Ed said with a grin. "He'll calm down once he realizes you're human. The Eagle Catcher has an awesome reputation, you know."

"Thanks to your big mouth and wild stories."

"Shucks, darlin' boy, I never said a word that wasn't fact. I flew your wing in 'Nam. There is nobody that handles a jet fighter like the Eagle Catcher. Nobody. I'm tellin' you, Jace, if you can't get this X-82 to fly, then it was meant to be a flowerpot for the general's wife. I want to see that baby soar into the wild blue yonder."

"Believe me, Ed, so do I!" Jace said adamantly, pulling the stack of folders toward him. "Let's see what you've done so far."

"I'll leave you to it," Ed said, getting to his feet. "Holler if you need me."

"Mmmm," Jace murmured, already deeply engrossed in the material in front of him.

* * *

When Heather entered her apartment that evening she headed straight for the shower. Afterward she sat at her dressing table and blow-dried her hair into feathery curls that fanned her cheeks, then applied blush, mascara, lipstick, and a smoky green eye shadow.

Her dress was a soft green wool with long sleeves and a matching belt that emphasized her tiny waist. Two thin gold chains adorned the round neckline, and black patent leather shoes with three-inch heels completed her ensemble. She was also wearing a smile.

She felt as though she were going to the prom, she thought as she sprayed a light cologne over her throat. She was definitely looking forward to the evening ahead. More precisely, she was eager to see Jace Dalton. How silly she'd been all day, with her whimsical sighs and daydreaming. But, oh, it felt good!

When a knock sounded at the door she glanced at her watch. He was fifteen minutes early. She hurried to the door and opened it.

"Hello, dear," one of her neighbors, Mrs. Hanson, said. "I brought back those books I borrowed. Oh, you look lovely. Are you going out?"

"Yes," Heather said, smiling. "Did you enjoy the books?"

"Oh, I certainly did."

"Why don't you come in, Mrs. Hanson, and select some more?"

"Not if you're busy, dear."

"I have a few minutes."

"All right then."

Jace pulled into his parking space and turned off the ignition. Damn, he thought as he strode around to the front of the building. He was running late. He'd lost all track of time once he'd started studying those files. He crossed the lobby and punched the button for the elevator. If the manager of the building had let the guy in to install his phone, he'd call Heather as soon as he got to his apartment and tell her he'd be there as quickly as possible. Fast shower, clean clothes—*civilian* clothes—and he'd be ready. Where in the hell was the elevator?

"These books look yummy," Mrs. Hanson said. "Thank you, Heather, and have a marvelous time tonight."

"I'm sure I will," Heather said, stepping out into the hall with Mrs. Hanson. "That historical is exciting. I hope you like it."

"I know I will. Oh, look, there's that handsome colonel getting out of the elevator. I spoke to him in the parking lot this morning. Hello, colonel," she called.

Damn it to hell! Jace thought, coming to a complete stop in the hallway.

Heather turned to look. "Oh, God, no!" she whispered.

"Well, good night now," Mrs. Hanson said, walking down the hall. "Thank you for the books."

Jace snapped out of his state of shock and strode toward Heather. Her eyes were wide and the color had drained from her face.

"Heather," he said when he was almost to her door, "I—"

"No!" she cried, backing up and starting to push the door closed.

Jace's arm shot out and caught the door, forcing it open. He entered Heather's apartment and closed the door behind him.

"Heather, I can explain—"

"Damn you!" she said, moving farther back as she wrapped her arms about herself in a protective gesture. "Why? Why did you lie to me? What sick game are you playing?"

"I'm not playing a game!" he growled. "That's the point, Heather. I was trying to do this right, give you a chance to—"

"Right? You call lying to me right? Dear Lord, silver wings! You're even a pilot. A damn pilot! What do you fly? A Buff? My, my, what a coincidence."

"No, I don't fly a Buff. I'm a test pilot. I—"

"Oh, really?" she said with a sharp, bitter laugh. "The darlings of the Air Force, isn't that what they call you? You test jockeys don't wait for death, you taunt it, dare it to smash your plane into smithereens. That's where the thrill comes in, doesn't it? Tempting death by flying an aircraft that may or may not hold together?"

"Heather, stop it! Listen to me!"

"Get out, colonel! Get out of my home and my life," she said, tears clinging to her lashes. "You have nothing to say that I want to hear. Your idea of a joke is cruel and hateful. Just go and leave me alone!"

"Dammit, no!" He closed the distance between them and grabbed her by the upper arms. "You're going to listen to what I have to say!"

"No, I'm not," she said, pushing against the unyielding wall of his chest. "I've heard all your lies." A sob caught in her throat and tears spilled onto her cheeks.

"Don't cry, Heather," Jace said, a haunting pain filling his heart. "Please don't cry." He gathered her close to him.

No! Heather's mind screamed. No! No! This wasn't Jace. This was a pilot. A pilot! But Jace was holding her in his arms. He was warm and strong, and . . .

With a strangled sob, she wrapped her arms around his waist and rested her head on his chest, drinking in the feel of his solid body. He lifted one hand to her head, combing his fingers through her silky curls as he held her, simply held her.

"Heather," he said. "Oh, Heather, I'm sorry."

"Don't do this to me, Jace," she whispered. "Please don't do this to me."

"Come on," he said gently. "Let's sit down. We've got to talk."

"No, I—"

"Shhh." He led her to the sofa and pulled her

down next to him. He took off his cap and set it on the cushion beside him, then shifted to face her. "Heather, I was going to tell you tonight that I'm an Air Force pilot. I would have preferred to wait longer, but I couldn't keep up the charade. I wanted you to get to know me, the man, and not be prejudiced by the uniform."

"Jace—"

"Hear me out, okay? Something happened when I met you, Heather. You knocked me over with your big brown eyes. You're there with me every minute, everywhere I go. You've churned up emotions in me that I've never felt before, and when I hold you, kiss you, I don't want to let you go. You've built walls around yourself that seem pretty high, but I told myself I'd get through them somehow. I thought that if we could have some time together you'd accept me as a man, and then we could face these other problems. I'm sorry if I hurt you. I was trying to do what I thought was best, and I guess I blew it. Don't shut me out, Heather. Don't rob us of what we might have because of this uniform. Please, Heather, give us a chance."

She saw his deep frown, heard the sincerity and the slightly frantic edge to his voice. But other voices were screaming in Heather's mind, demanding her attention, making her listen to the echoes of the past. Russ's death in the fiery crash of the B-52. Russ, who had worn the blue uniform and chosen to fly—to fly until it killed him.

"Heather?" Jace said softly.

"I'm just so frightened," she said, looking

directly into his gentle eyes. "I can't think straight. I've been so happy since I met you, Jace. I'd forgotten what it was like to smile, really smile, and when you kiss me . . . When I saw you in that uniform it was déjà vu, a nightmare replaying in my mind. I don't know what to do. You just came into my life and I don't want you to leave. I don't! But, Jace, you're a pilot, a test pilot. I can't handle it. I can't deal with the game of roulette you play with death every time you get into one of those planes." She shook her head. "I feel as though I'm being pulled in two. Half of me wants you here with me so badly, and the other wants to scream and demand you leave me in peace."

"It's too late, don't you see?" he said. "We can't pretend that what's happening between us isn't there. You've become very important to me very quickly, and from what you're saying, you feel something for me too."

"Yes," she said slowly. "I do."

"Heather, this is a uniform of the Air Force, not one of death. People die every day in automobile accidents, but we get into our cars and drive anyway. Life doesn't stop because of one tragic incident. I've flown planes for twenty years. I'm very much alive and intend to stay that way."

"But you don't know that you will."

"Do *you*? Can you guarantee me that I won't lose you to a freak accident or to illness? Can you?"

"No, I guess not."

"We're talking about life here, Heather, with all its unknowns. Some of the hands we get dealt are lousy, but others are fantastic. You, me, together, we're on the edge of the fantastic. Don't throw it away because of the past. We'll take it slow and easy. You'll have all the time you need to adjust to this uniform, my job. I'll answer your questions, tell you exactly what I'm doing."

"You said your work was classified."

"No, the X-82 jet isn't classified. The public knows about it, if they're interested enough to read the newspapers. Heather, will you try it? One step at a time? One day at a time? It's up to you. I can't—won't—force myself on you. If you want me to leave, I'll go, and I'll never bother you again."

Heather pushed herself to her feet and walked across the room to stare, unseeing, at the books in the bookcase. She pressed her fingertips to her aching temples and tried desperately to sort through the maze in her mind.

Send Jace away? Never see him again? Never again be held in his strong arms, feel his lips on hers? No! No, she didn't want him to go. But, oh Lord, where would she get the strength, the courage, to face each day, not knowing if death would claim him? He flew those planes, those damnable planes that held him captive like shiny metal coffins. But tell him to go? Let him disappear from her life as quickly as he had come? How could she smile, really smile, without Jace?

"Jace." She turned to face him. "I don't want you to leave me. I'll cry if you do, and I really hate to cry. But you have to understand how frightened I am, and realize I just may not have the courage to face the world you live in. I just don't know if I can. I'll try, one day at a time, like you said."

Jace stared at the ceiling for a long minute. He let out a deep breath, only then realizing he had hardly been breathing while waiting for Heather to speak. He stood up and walked toward her, stopping a few steps away and extending his hand.

"Thank you," he said, his voice hushed. "You're not alone anymore, Heather. I'm here now, with you. I'll never intentionally do anything to hurt you or make you cry."

She tentatively lifted her hand and stepped forward to place it in Jace's. Their eyes met and held in a timeless moment. The warmth from their hands seemed to weave together, joining them, making them one. Slowly, slowly, the embers of desire grew to a blazing fire that threatened to consume them.

"Heather," Jace groaned, then gathered her into his embrace and kissed her.

She went limp in his arms, leaning against him for support as she answered the rough demands of his lips and tongue. His fingers wove through her hair to bring her nearer as their tongues met and twined in the sweet darkness of her mouth. She felt him shudder with desire, felt him strive for control, but she lacked the strength to move away from his body. His tongue plummeted deeper, deeper, as if seeking the path to her soul, and a moan escaped her.

"Oh, Heather," Jace murmured, his voice vibrant with passion as he moved her gently away from him, "I want you so much. So damn much. You've cast a spell over me, Heather Wade." He took a deep breath. "Listen, I promised you dinner. Give me a few minutes to shower and change, then we'll go out to eat. You look very pretty in that dress and I want to show you off. Besides that . . ."

She smiled. "You're hungry."

"There it is, the smile. Twenty minutes and I'll be back." He brushed his lips over hers. "Okay?"

"Yes, okay," she said as he snatched his cap from the sofa and strode out the door.

But nothing was okay, she thought an instant later. Was she falling in love with Jace Dalton? Love seemed to be hovering just out of her emotional reach at the moment, taunting her, teasing her with thoughts of life without him, now that he had touched her world. She had only to envision his leaving to feel the emptiness wash over her in an icy wave of misery.

Perhaps she already loved him, but the fear of that love was too great to allow her to admit it to her inner self. Whether she was a breath away from being in love with Jace or already there didn't matter, because it was wrong, totally wrong. She didn't want to relinquish her soul to a man, not again. And, dear heaven, she didn't want to love a man who wore a uniform, who was a pilot, a tempter of death.

"No!" she said, pressing her hands to her cheeks. "I won't fall in love with him. I can't!"

With a weary sigh, she walked into the bathroom, splashed water on her tear-stained face, and repaired her makeup.

Now what? she asked herself. Now she would wait for Jace to return. That was how it worked. The man left, the woman waited and waited. There was nothing equal or fair about a life centered on a man who marched to the cadence of the military drum. But how did she stop it, this seed of caring for Jace Dalton? How did she keep it from growing until it was so enormous it consumed her?

Jace stepped into the shower and let the stinging water beat against his body. He was coiled with tension, every muscle tight and aching. He felt as though he had just pleaded for his life and had been granted a stay of execution for an undetermined length of time. His relationship with Heather was fragile, as delicate as whisper-thin crystal, and could shatter into a million fragments at any moment. He didn't want that to happen. *He did not want to lose Heather Wade!*

He stepped from the shower and dried himself quickly. Heather was so frightened, he thought as he strode into the bedroom. Her eyes did remind him of a fawn's, and she herself was like that gentle animal—skittish, wary, afraid to trust. Love had brought her only pain in the past. He would have to enter her world slowly, carefully. Inch by emotional inch he would teach her to trust and believe in him.

Jace knotted a brown tie and straightened the

collar of the tan shirt he wore with brown slacks. Brown, he thought, shrugging into his sports coat. Good. Heather had seen quite enough of him in blue for one day.

Minutes later he knocked lightly on her door. When she opened it he looked intently at her pale face.

"Are you all right?" he asked, stepping into the apartment.

"Yes . . . No . . . I don't know," she said, throwing up her hands.

"That's a very firm, very decisive reply."

"Like it?" she said, smiling slightly. "It's the only one I have at the moment."

"It'll do for now. Let's go have dinner."

"Jace, are you going to tell me what the X-82 is?"

"Only if you want to know."

"You're being very nice to me."

"I'm a nice guy. Let's eat."

"Aren't you awfully young to be a colonel?"

"No, Heather, I'm not, but I'm too young to die of starvation."

"Oh. We'd better go then."

"Thank you."

"I'll say this much for your uniform. It does wonderful things for your blue eyes."

He laughed and shook his head. "Get your coat, Heather."

Why? Heather wondered as they rode down in the elevator. Why wasn't she afraid of anything when she was with Jace? Was that because she was already counting on him to make her able to function? Oh, she just couldn't think about it anymore tonight. Not tonight. She just wanted to be with Jace and push everything else to a dusty corner of her mind.

"I'm rather hungry myself," she said.

Jace smiled and circled her shoulders with his arm, pulling her close to his side and kissing her on the temple.

"You smell good," he said.

"So do you. All soapy and fresh. Where were you stationed in Michigan?"

"Sawyer. Is your hair naturally curly?"

"Yes. Are you a good pilot, Jace?"

"One of the best. Is your perfume rose-scented?"

"Lilacs, like my soap. Why do they call a test pilot the man with the golden arm?"

"It's because we make superb takeoffs and landings, my sweet. Your skin is so soft."

"Jace, quit nibbling on my ear!"

"I told you I was hungry. You, Ms. Wade, are delicious!"

Their laughter danced through the clear, cold night air as they left the building and walked to Jace's car. Forty-five minutes later they were seated in a cozy restaurant, sipping wine. A candle flickered in the center of the table, casting a golden glow over both of them. Jace held Heather's hand, stroking it gently with his thumb.

"A lifetime has passed since I met you, Heather," he said, looking directly into her eyes. "I feel as though I've known you forever. Or maybe it's that I've been waiting for you for that long and didn't even know it. But you're here now with me, and that's where I want you to stay."

"One day at a time, Jace," she said quietly.

"For now. I won't rush you. At least, I'll try my damnedest not to. Don't be afraid of me, pretty fawn. I'm not going to hurt you."

"I don't think you would intend to, but—"

"Enough heavy talk. Change the subject."

"Tell me about the X-82."

"You don't have to take that on tonight, Heather. We could do childhoods and favorite movies."

"No, I want to know why you're here, what you're supposed to do."

"The X-82 is a new fighter jet, and at the moment it's in trouble."

"Why?"

He chuckled. "It won't fly. Other than that, it's a beautiful machine."

"What's wrong with it?"

"Beats me. That's what I'm here to find out."

"They brought you all the way from Sawyer to figure out what's what with this plane?"

"Yep."

"My goodness, that's very impressive, colonel."

"Well, thank you, ma'am."

"What if you can't fix it?"

"I'll fix it."

"Jace, are you conceited?"

"No, just confident. That plane is going to fly."

"Who—who is going to fly it?"

"Heather, don't. I can see you tensing up."

"Who?"

"I will."

"Oh, Jace."

"Listen to me. There's a prototype here. We'll put that plane through a hundred flights on the simulator before I go up. The X-82 is just sitting there looking pretty. Hey, being a test pilot isn't all glamour and glory. I've got a helluva lot of tedious hours ahead of me, messing around with computers and printouts. The X-82 is a long way from leaving the ground with me in it."

"I see."

"You'll know when I'm going to fly it, Heather, because I'll tell you. I don't intend to keep anything from you."

"And you're a good pilot?"

"Yes, Heather, I'm a very good pilot."

"Have you ever made any mistakes when you were flying, Jace?"

"Mistakes? Like what?"

"I don't know really. I—Oh, here's our dinner. At last you can eat."

"And I'm ready," he said, smiling, but inside he was troubled. Heather kept asking whether or not he was a good pilot. Why? He hadn't made any mistakes that mattered, because he was still alive. Big mistakes killed pilots. What was Heather really trying to find out?

As they enjoyed their steak dinners Jace steered the conversation to lighter topics. He asked Heather about her family, and she told him her parents lived in Scottsdale, just outside of

Phoenix, and were presently on a long-dreamed-of cruise.

"Arranged by Wishing Well Travel, I presume," he said.

"But, of course, sir."

Jace told her of his father, a retired Air Force general who lived in Virginia, and of his married sister and her family in Florida. They shared stories of their childhoods, and laughed at the youthful pranks they had played. Over coffee Heather explained her long friendship with Lori, and how they had come to start the travel agency.

"You two should be very proud of what you've accomplished," Jace said.

"Yes, we are." She suddenly leaned forward and smiled. "You know, the way the candlelight is flickering, those few strands of gray in your hair are glowing like silver. Very distinguished."

He chuckled. "You like that, huh? I earned every one of those gray hairs. They're mine to keep. The X-82 will probably give me a few more before I'm done."

"You're very excited about this project, aren't you?"

"It's a tremendous challenge, Heather. To have been chosen to try to salvage this thing is an honor I'm not taking lightly. I don't like to fail, and I don't intend to. That plane wasn't built by idiots. There's a reason it isn't functioning, and I'll find out what it is. The X-82 is going to fly."

Heather heard the fierce determination in Jace's voice, saw the glimmer in his blue eyes. He wouldn't rest until that plane was in the air. Jace Dalton accomplished what he set out to do. The Air Force had obviously chosen well when they had brought him in. He was a top-notch pilot and a credit to his uniform. But what of Jace Dalton the man? Did he tackle his personal life with the same intention to succeed? Did he see *her* as an uncompleted mission, a goal? Did her fear of loving, her aversion to the Air Force and planes, spark his competitive instincts? Did he view her as a woman, or merely as a challenge?

"Heather?" Jace asked. "Are you in there?"

"What? Oh, I was thinking."

"About?"

"You."

"Uh-oh. Am I in trouble?"

"You're a very intense, complicated man, Jace. You said yourself that you don't like to fail, and so you don't. You accomplish whatever it is you've set out to do."

"I don't see anything wrong with that."

"No, of course not. It's a very admirable trait except . . . Well, people aren't planes."

"Really?" He grinned. "That's a nifty news flash. Am I missing a message here?"

"Have you ever had any difficulty getting the woman of your choice?"

"Do we really want to discuss this topic?" he asked, frowning slightly.

"Have you?"

"No, I suppose not. But what . . . Oh, now wait a minute. This scenario you're putting together is becoming clear. There's a plane that needs flying, and the fly boy makes sure it flies. He crooks his finger, and the women tumble into his bed. And then, lo and behold, he comes across a woman who says, 'No, thanks, Jace. I don't want to get involved with you or your crummy planes.' 'Well now,' says the colonel, 'we'll just see about that, because it's like dropping a gauntlet and daring me to pick it up.' Is that what you're thinking, Heather?"

"Well, it occurred to me that maybe you view me as a—a challenge."

"Hold it," he said. He shook his head, then picked up her hand and cradled it between both of his. "It could appear that way, I guess, except for one very important fact that you're not aware of." And that he hadn't been aware of up until a few moments ago. He felt a warmth glowing deep inside him, felt his smile widen with pure pleasure.

"And that is?" Heather asked.

"And that is that I'm in love with you, Heather Wade. I am very deeply in love with you. You are not a temporary assignment, a challenge for the here and now. I'm dealing in forever, and I've never done that before. I love you. I want you. But even more, I need you in my life, close, with me. You are loved, Heather, and now I have to figure out how to convince you to love me in return."

Four

Heather couldn't breathe. The air seemed to swish from her lungs. When she opened her mouth to speak nothing came out, and she clamped it closed again. She stared at Jace as though he had just landed on earth from an alien planet.

"Heather," he said, his voice low, "don't be frightened. Everything is going to be wonderful. I love you. I do love you so very much."

That did it.

Heather burst into tears.

"Oh, good Lord," Jace said, "now I've done it. Heather, don't cry, okay?"

"Oh-h-h," she wailed, burying her face in her hands.

"Waiter! Check!"

After paying the bill, Jace hustled a sniffling

Heather out of the restaurant, smiling weakly at the frowning hostess. Outside, he helped Heather into the car, then ran around to the driver's side and slid behind the wheel.

"Heather?" he said gently. "Talk to me."

"I . . ." She took a wobbly breath. "I don't want you to love me."

"Why not?" he asked, turning her by the shoulders to face him.

"Because if you love me I'll have to get in touch with myself as to how I feel about you, and I think I'm falling in love with you, but I didn't check to make sure, because I really didn't want to know, because I don't want to love you, but it's probably too late, and you fly airplanes, and wear a uniform, and I can't handle that either, and—oh-h-h," she cried, and the tears started again.

"Heather, Heather," he said, pulling her into his arms, "you think maybe, just maybe, that you're falling in love with me? That's fantastic! Great! Unbelievable!"

"It's terrible!" she said, burying her face in his jacket.

"It's wonderful!"

"It's awful!"

Jace laughed, causing Heather's head to bob up and down on his chest.

"This is a rather crazy conversation here," he said. "Heather, we'll work everything out together, don't you see?"

"No!"

"Look at me."

"No!"

"Heather, look at me," he said firmly.

She slowly lifted her head and gazed up at him. The moon had cast a silvery luminescence over the interior of the car, and her tears glistened like dewdrops on her cheeks. Jace cupped her face in his hands and wiped the moisture away with his thumbs. Her eyes were wide and frightened, and his heart beat a strange tattoo in his chest.

Look at her, he thought. So scared, so fragile and vulnerable. And she was close to loving him! She was! He'd make her understand that there was nothing to fear. She wouldn't lose herself by loving him. She was different from that young bride of years ago, and she would come to realize that. He wouldn't rob her of anything—he'd give her all he had. As for the Air Force, the planes, he'd carefully ease her back into that world, show her it was simply his job, not a miscreant force waiting to take his life. They were together now, and he wasn't going to let her go!

"Heather," he said, "I realize you have misgivings about loving, and about the Air Force, but we can deal with all that if we do it together."

"Oh, Jace, I don't know what to do, or think, or say. A part of me is so incredibly happy that you love me, and another is angry that you've destroyed my resolve to just be me, alone, in charge of my own life. I'm terribly confused and—Ouch!"

"Ouch?"

"The gear shift is poking a hole in my leg."

"Oh, sorry." He lifted her back onto the bucket

seat. "Damned sports car. Listen, you're all worn out. I'll take you home so you can get a good night's sleep. Everything will be clearer in the morning."

"No, it won't."

"Yes, it will."

"No!"

He chuckled as he turned the key in the ignition. "Let's not start doing that number again."

Heather sighed and leaned her head back. Jace loved her, she thought. Oh, glory be, he did! But she *did* feel torn in two. Jace was everything she wanted and everything she didn't want. He was heaven and hell in a six-foot-plus package. She felt drained, and her brain was turning into shredded wheat. She'd sleep for five years, then see how she felt about all of this.

At the apartment building Jace parked the car, then led Heather inside to the elevator. He held her hand tightly in his, and she felt like a child being escorted home after an evening out with the grown-ups. In her living room he helped her off with her coat, then stepped back, shoving his hands into his pockets.

"You . . . um, better get to bed," he said.

"Would you like a drink or something?"

"No, I'll go and leave you alone. You've had a lot hit you all at once, and you probably need a little private time to sort it all out. Just don't think too much tonight, okay? Get some sleep first, then look at it fresh in the morning. I love you. Concentrate on that for now."

"Yes, all right."

"I don't think I should kiss you, Heather."

"Why not?"

"Because for the first time in my life I'm in love. If I touched you right now, I'm not sure I could let you go. I want to make love to you, become one with you. You're my lady, my love, my life. I've never felt this way before, and I can't vouch for my control at the moment."

She gazed up at him and saw the muscle twitching in his jaw, the coiled tension of his body, the beads of perspiration on his brow. He was staring at a spot somewhere above her head, and she realized how difficult it must have been to admit his lack of total command of himself. He was being so honest with her, at the cost of his pride. Before she knew she was moving she had stepped close to him, encircled his waist with her arms, and leaned her head on his chest.

"Oh, Heather, don't," he said, his voice strained as he kept his hands in his pockets. "I can't handle having you next to me. Not tonight."

Tears of confusion and exhaustion misted her eyes as she stepped back and looked up at him. She swallowed the lump in her throat and attempted a weak smile that failed. A single tear slid down her cheek.

"Oh, hell," he said with a strangled moan.

He pulled her roughly into his arms and brought his mouth down hard on hers. In the next instant, though, the kiss softened into a gentle, sensuous embrace, and a sob escaped Heather's throat. She wrapped her arms around his neck and answered the demands of his tongue, parting her lips to its thrust. He groaned deep in his chest as he drank of her sweetness, his tongue dipping in rhythmic motions that matched the pulsing heat in the secret place of her femininity. Her fingers burrowed into his thick hair, urging him closer, closer, as the kiss grew urgent, frenzied.

His hands slid to her buttocks, fitting her to his rugged contours, his arousal pressing hard against her in a bold announcement of his need. The liquid fire of passion poured through Heather's body. Her knees trembled, and she clung to Jace for support. Time lost its meaning, as did reality and reason. She was awash with desire. She wanted, needed, ached for Jace to bring to her the promise of his masculinity.

"Heather!" Jace gasped, gripping her by the upper arms and jerking her away from him.

"I want you," she whispered. "I want you to make love to me."

"No!" he said, raking his hand through his hair. "I can't! Not tonight. I don't want our lovemaking to get jumbled up with the fears and confusion you're dealing with right now. It's too much, too fast for you. Oh, Heather, don't you see? I'm scared to death of losing you. If we take this step too soon, you may come to hate me for rushing you into something you weren't emotionally ready for. I'm not trying to make your decisions for you. I swear I'm not. All I know is, I can't make love to you tonight."

"All—all right," she said, looking down at the floor.

"Hey." He tilted her chin up. "Get some sleep. I'll see you tomorrow. I have to be out at the base early, but I'll come over as soon as I get home. Okay?"

"Okay, Jace."

" 'Night," he said, brushing his lips over hers. "I love you."

He walked to the door, then turned, gazing at her with a slight frown. After a moment he left the apartment, shutting the door behind him.

"He loves me," she said softly. "I'm the happiest, and the unhappiest, person in the world."

With one last sniffle, she turned out the lights and walked slowly and wearily into the bedroom.

The next morning Ed Turner entered Jace's office to find Jace sitting in his chair, staring at the ceiling, fingers laced behind his head.

"The Thinker," Ed said. "Coffee hot?"

"Yeah."

"Any clues yet as to the problem with the X-82?"

"Nope."

"Do you have some sort of attack plan here?"

"Yeah."

"That's nice. You sure are talkative this morning. I guess you're really concentrating on that plane, huh?"

"Nope. I'm not on duty yet. Colonel Dalton doesn't show up for another half hour."

"Oh, that's interesting," Ed said, sitting down opposite the desk. "Who am I chatting with?"

"*Jace* Dalton."

"Got it. How's life, Jace?"

"I'm in love."

Ed choked on his coffee and coughed until his face turned red.

"You're what?" he croaked.

"I'm in love," Jace said, dropping his hands and grinning at Ed. "How do you like that, kid?"

"This is a joke, right? Jace Dalton, who needs a big stick to beat off the women, has gone over the edge, taken the dive, crashed and burned?"

"Yep," Jace said, looking quite pleased with himself.

"I'll be damned." Ed smiled. "What's her name?"

"Heather."

"And? Are you getting married? Having babies? The whole nine yards?"

"Well, there're a few problems I've got to work through."

"Like what?"

"Heather really doesn't want to be in love. She also has a thing about the Air Force. She's not real crazy about the uniform, you know what I mean? And she hates planes, is petrified of being involved with a pilot."

"Well, golly gee, darlin' boy, is that all that's wrong? Hell, Jace, you've got a whole deck stacked against you. You could have had the pick of the litter. Why did you choose someone who—"

"I love her, Ed," Jace said quietly.

"Yeah. Yeah, I can see that. I sure as hell hope you can solve the little, minor, small, minuscule things you've got going against you there. Why doesn't she want to be in love with you? You're a lovable guy, aren't you?"

"Heather was married to a Buff pilot who was killed. She was very young, lived her entire life for the man. She sort of lost herself when he died. She sees love as a threat to her identity. Put that together with an Air Force pilot husband who wiped himself out and . . . Get the picture?"

"Whew! Heavy stuff. You've got a road to go, Jace, but you'll figure it out. The Eagle Catcher is awesome in action. Man, this is unreal. The Eagle Catcher has been caught. I'd say the name belongs to Heather now."

Jace chuckled. "She's got me, all right."

"I'm happy for you, darlin' boy. I sure hope it all works out."

"It'll fly, Ed. I've made up my mind. Do you still have some connections from when you were stationed at Langley?"

"Sure. Why?"

"Could you get me a copy of the investigation of the crash of a Buff three years ago that was piloted by a Russ, probably Russell, Wade? I don't know his rank."

"I imagine I can. Why?"

"I don't know. I'd just like to see what the circumstances were surrounding Heather's husband's death. He went down in a storm, so it's probably open and shut, but . . ."

"I'll make a call."

"Thanks."

"When do I get to meet this pretty little Eagle Catcher?"

"Soon, I hope. You'll like her. She's fantastic."

When Heather entered Wishing Well Travel she found a weeping Lori.

"Lori!" she exclaimed. "What's wrong?"

"I—I had an early appointment this morning and—Oh, Heather, I'm pregnant!"

"What?" Heather said. "Really? Oh, Lori, that's wonderful!"

"I know. I can't believe it! I never even suspected because I've always had a very irregular cycle. And now I'm going to have a baby! Me! Oh, and Jerry, of course. Jerry! I've got to tell him. No, not on the phone. It's too special for that. Oh, Heather, I'm so happy."

The two women hugged each other tightly, then launched into an animated discussion about colors for the nursery, whether Lori should enroll in natural childbirth classes, and guesses as to whether it would be a boy or a girl. Lori called Jerry at work and invited him out to lunch, then left the office at noon with a lovely smile on her face.

"A baby," Heather murmured. "That's so nice." She had wanted a baby, but Russ had said there was plenty of time for a family later. He didn't want to share her, he had said. But *she* had shared *him*. He was gone continually, and had admitted that he was away much of the time because he had volunteered. It would look good on his record when he came up for promotion, he would say. And there she had sat, waiting for him to come home. Waiting and waiting. And Jace? Had they been able to have breakfast together this morning? No, of course not, because he had to get to the base and see his plane. And there she sat waiting once again.

At four o'clock Jace stood with his arms crossed over his chest and a scowl on his face, staring at the paper spread across the table.

Damn, he thought, there had to be an answer somewhere in that mumbo jumbo. The specs for the X-82 had been drawn by experts. The plane had been built by experts. His crew was made up of experts. So why wouldn't the damn thing fly?

"Colonel Dalton, sir?" Bruce said, coming up behind him.

"Yes?"

"Well, sir, I . . . um . . . They called and said . . . You see, sir . . ."

"Spit it out, Bruce!"

"Oh. Yes, sir. You're an hour short on your high-altitude proficiency flights."

"I know."

"You do? Oh, thank goodness." Bruce let out a long breath. "I thought you'd be really burned up because you had to take time off from the X-82 to mess around doing what everybody already knows you can do."

"I never complain about flying an airplane," Jace said, slapping Bruce on the shoulder. "Oh, sorry," he added when the airman staggered slightly. "Didn't mean to knock you over."

"No problem, sir. I'm used to taking my lumps. I've always been on the small side."

"Size isn't that important, Bruce."

"Easy for you to say. Guys built like you have it made because—Excuse me, sir. Didn't mean to be disrespectful."

"You weren't. Bruce, why did you join the Air Force?"

"Off the record, sir?"

"Absolutely."

"Because I thought maybe if I were wearing the same uniform as everyone else, I would be accepted as an equal. Didn't work, though. I still get razzed about my size."

"They could be jealous, you know. You're involved in a very important project here."

"Yeah, well, that fell through the first time the guys in my barracks asked me what the X-82 looked like, and I had to say I'd never seen it."

"What do you mean, you've never seen it? You have clearance to go in that hangar."

"Yes, sir, but I have to stay here to answer the phone."

"Oh," Jace said thoughtfully. "I guess someone has to man the phones."

"Yes, sir. Anyway, about your high altitude . . ."

"See if you can schedule it for 0-eight hundred Monday."

"I'll call them right now," Bruce said, saluting crisply.

"Bruce, if I return every salute you give me, I won't have enough strength left in my arm to get a plane off the ground. When we're alone just let it go, okay?"

"I think that's against regulations, sir. 'When in the presence of a superior officer'—"

"I've read the handbook. Trust me. No one will know."

"Yes, sir. Thank you, sir. I'll go make that call."

"Nice kid," Jace said under his breath as Bruce left the office.

Jace was still frowning at the papers when Bruce returned a few minutes later.

"You're all set for 0-eight hundred Monday, sir."

"Good. The weather was so lousy at Sawyer before I left, I couldn't get my flight time in. What's my tower code?"

"Eagle Catcher. It had already been filed."

Jace chuckled. "Major Turner strikes again. Okay, Bruce, take off. That's it for today."

"Are you leaving, sir?"

"Not yet."

"I'd be glad to stay in case you need anything."

"No, but thanks anyway."

"Well, good night, sir."

Bruce started to salute, then dropped his hand back to his side and walked slowly from the room. Jace watched him leave, his dark brows knitted together. He strode into his office, picked up the phone, and called personnel.

"This is Colonel Dalton on the X-82 project," he said. "I need a secretary assigned to me from the pool . . . Yeah, I know you show me listed as having an aide, but I want him freed up to work with me in the hangar. . . . Fine. Monday morning. Thank you." He hung up the phone. "Let's see if we can't get you to grow a little bit taller, Bruce," he said quietly.

Three hours later Jace was walking down the hall to his apartment. He stopped, studied his uniform for a moment, then went on to Heather's door, knocking lightly.

"Jace!" she said an instant later as she flung open the door. "Hi, come in. Guess what?"

"What?" he asked as he stepped into the apartment. His gaze flickered appreciatively over her designer jeans and fluffy pink sweater.

"Lori is going to have a baby!"

"Lori? Lori. Oh, Lori! Your partner at the travel agency. I take it everyone is pleased about it?"

"Thrilled! They'd just about given up hope it would ever happen. Lori took Jerry out to lunch and told him. She said he just about passed out, and that he bought cigars and took them back to his office. I'm just so happy for them."

"I can tell," he said, tossing his cap onto the sofa and pulling her into his arms. "Your eyes are sparkling. I love seeing you like this. In fact, I love everything about you."

"Hello, Jace," she said, wrapping her arms around his neck.

"Hello, my Heather."

Their kiss was sweet and sensuous, and it went on and on. Heather pressed her soft body against Jace as their tongues met and drew lazy circles around each other. Her heart was beating wildly as tingling fingers of desire crept through her. She drank in the taste of Jace Dalton, his strength, his heat, his special aroma, savoring all of him.

He finally lifted his head and took a steadying breath. "You're nice to come home to, Heather," he said.

She smiled. "So are you, Jace."

"Would you like to go out to dinner?"

"I just put chicken in the oven. There's plenty, if you'd like to stay."

"I don't expect you to cook for me," he said, then grinned. "But that chicken does smell good. I'll have to go to the grocery store later to supply my kitchen. I'll go change my clothes now. No, I'll kiss you again, then go change."

He kissed her passionately, then left her apartment with a promise to be back in a flash. After he had gone Heather drew a long breath, waited for her heart to return to a quiet rhythm, then walked into the kitchen and set the table for two.

Table for two, she thought. Chicken in the oven. How domesticated and normal. They'd share the events of their day, chat, clean up the kitchen together like a married couple. But they weren't like other couples. Jace flew planes—and could die, just like Russ.

She shivered, then pushed the distressing thought from her mind as she began to make a salad. A few minutes later she heard a knock and hurried to the door. Jace was dressed in faded jeans that hugged his hips and thighs and a black sweater that accentuated the raven glow of his hair. He pulled her to him and kissed her deeply before either said a word.

"Very nice," he said, when he finally released her. "Maybe I'll go out and come in again. This could become habit-forming."

Heather laughed in delight, then led Jace into the kitchen. He leaned against the counter while she finished the salad.

"What with Lori's news, I guess you had a good day," he said, picking up a piece of cucumber and popping it into his mouth.

"Yes, I did." She paused, then added thoughtfully, "I had a very good day. I wasn't just sitting around waiting for you. I'm a businesswoman with my own business. I have a reason for being separate from . . . well . . ."

"From the man in your life?" Jace said. "That's what I've been trying to tell you, Heather. You've grown since the time you were married. You'll never lose your identity again by loving. You just wouldn't allow it to happen, don't you see?"

"I'm beginning to," she said, nodding slowly.

"It's all going to come together for us, Heather."

"How was *your* day, Jace?"

"Nothing exciting. The X-82 crew thinks I have a screw loose. I sent my aide over to the commissary for six feet of butcher paper and color felt pens. We're making a master chart of all the computer printouts. It's very slow, tedious work."

"And you have no clue as to what's wrong with the X-82?"

"Not yet. Heather, Monday morning I have an hour of high-altitude proficiency flying to do. Anyone observing it won't see more than the takeoff and landing. I'd like you to come out and watch."

Five

"No, Jace!" Heather cried, the paring knife in her hand clattering onto the counter.

"A takeoff and landing," he said, gripping her shoulders. "That's all. It's a start. We have to begin somewhere, and this is short and sweet. The plane goes up, then comes down. I'll ask my friend Ed Turner to stay with you while I'm flying. Will you do it?"

"I don't know," she said, her voice shaky.

"Think about it, okay? The fact that I'm a pilot isn't going to go away. You need to view it fresh again, see that it's mostly routine, nothing flashy or dangerous. All I'm asking is that you give it a fair chance, and Monday is an easy way to begin. Will you think about it?"

"Yes, I will."

"That's all I ask. Now, what can I do to help with this meal?"

"Make a pot of coffee, I guess."

"Yes, ma'am. Right away, ma'am."

Jace whistled, terribly off-key, as he set about his chore, and Heather returned her attention to the salad.

Watch Jace fly a plane? she thought. No, she didn't want to, did not want to see him crawl into that machine, then be carried far above the ground. No!

"Chicken's done," she said, taking the pan from the oven. "Are you all set?"

"Ready, ready now," he said.

Heather felt the color drain from her face, and she placed the pan on the counter with trembling hands.

"Don't say that," she said hoarsely.

"Don't say—Oh, damn!" Jace closed the distance between them and wrapped his arms around her. "I'm sorry. That's a B-52 slogan. I'm sorry, Heather."

"It shouldn't bother me after all this time. It's just been so long since I've heard it, and it took me off guard. Russ used it continually, for everything. 'Ready, ready now' seemed to apply to every aspect of his life. I got so sick of hearing it. It was like having a B-52 as a member of the family, always there, demanding something. Ready, ready now? Oh, yes, he was always ready to fly. Then he'd say it in our kitchen, the living room, even, dear heaven, our bedroom. I screamed at him once to never say it around me again, but he just laughed, said it was part of being married to a Buff pilot. But he said it over and over and—"

"Heather, don't," Jace said, tightening his hold on her. "You're only going to upset yourself."

"Oh, Jace, don't you see? I can't deal with any of this. They were only words, and they brought back so many memories. What do you think is going to happen when I watch you get into that plane? No! No, I can't do it. There's nothing in that world that I want or—"

"*I'm* in that world, Heather," he said quietly.

"Dammit, I know! Why do you think I feel so torn in two? I care for you, Jace, but I hate what you do. It's going to destroy us. My weaknesses are going to rob us of the happiness we might have had together."

"No! Don't even think that. Nothing is going to happen to us. Heather, come to the base Monday. Take that first small step. Please?"

"I—I just don't know."

"Give it a rest for now. Come on, let's eat before that chicken gets cold."

Despite the knot in her stomach, Heather nodded and carried the salad to the table. She concentrated on swallowing the food around the lump in her throat, and the meal was a tense, silent event. She could sense Jace looking at her, but refused to meet his gaze. Finally she gave up the effort to eat and pushed her plate away.

"I'll help you clean up," he said, getting to his feet.

"No, that's all right. You said you wanted to go to the grocery store."

"Are you saying you'd prefer to be alone?"

"I'm not very good company right now, Jace."

"Look, Heather . . ." He paused, then said, "Yeah, okay, I'll see you later."

Heather heard the front door close, then buried her face in her hands as the tears started to flow.

"No!" she said, standing. "I won't cry! I'm acting like a frightened child instead of a woman." She had to overcome her fears. She had to, or she was going to lose Jace before she even had the chance to find out if she was in love with him!

As Jace drove his hands gripped the steering wheel with much more force than was necessary. His jaw was set in a hard line and a muscle in his cheek was twitching.

Damn it! he thought. What was he going to do? He couldn't fight shadows, box with ghosts from the past. He didn't know how to beat the insidious forces that were holding Heather in an iron grip. A simple phrase like "Ready, ready now" had set her into a tailspin. He had the option of leaving the Air Force in six months, but even if he did, he'd want a civilian job that involved flying. Flying was a part of him, made him who he was. Damn, what a mess.

When Jace returned from the store it took him two trips to carry the groceries to his apartment. After putting everything away he stood in the middle of the living room and frowned.

Now what? he asked himself. Did he go back to Heather's and see if she had calmed down? No, maybe not. Maybe he'd pushed her too hard about coming to the base. Still, all it consisted of was her seeing a takeoff and landing. It couldn't get any more simple than that. If she wouldn't even agree to that much, then how in the hell were they going to make any headway in their relationship? He loved that woman! He wanted her to be a part of his life.

"Ah, hell!" he said, slouching on the sofa. "Why does it all have to be so complicated? I love her. Why isn't that enough?"

When Heather finished cleaning the kitchen she started in on the rest of the apartment, she dusted, vacuumed, rearranged the furniture, then put it all back the way it had been. She pushed her body and blanked out her mind. At last, exhausted, she took a long, hot bath, donned her nightgown, and crawled into bed. Only then did she admit she'd been listening for Jace's knock at the door the entire evening.

Well, she thought, staring up into the darkness, she couldn't blame him for staying away. She was acting so immature, it was nauseating. The man had said a common Air Force slogan and she'd come unhinged. Jace was moving so gently, so carefully. All he'd asked her to do was watch him take off and land, and she'd withdrawn behind her wall of fear, not allowing him to get close to her.

She had to find the courage to go to that base on Monday morning. She just had to!

Jace slept restlessly and woke with a headache that made him irritable. He consumed several cups of coffee, but they didn't help.

Had he made a mistake by not going back over to Heather's the previous night? he wondered as he drove to the base. Had he appeared angry, uncaring? He had decided that she needed some time alone, but who in the hell was he to know what she needed? There was nothing simple about this being in love stuff, that was for sure. He'd wanted to see her this morning, but it had been too early to go pounding on her door. What was she thinking? Had she cried after he'd left her? Damn.

" 'Morning, sir," Bruce said, saluting as Jace entered the office.

"Yeah. Any aspirin around here?"

"Yes, sir."

"Let me have a couple, will you?"

Bruce retrieved a bottle from the desk drawer and gave Jace two aspirin, then asked if he wanted a glass of water.

"No, thanks," Jace said. "Not if the coffee is ready."

"It's ready, sir."

"Good. Oh, listen, on Monday morning there will be a secretary coming over from the pool. I want you to train him or her to take over here, because when we go back to the hangar after charting this data, you're coming with us."

"Sir?" Bruce said, his eyes wide.

"I need you down there, Bruce. You'll be working directly with me and the crew on the X-82. Any questions?"

"No, sir. Thank you, sir. Oh, yes, sir!"

"Fine," Jace said, striding into his office. Well, at least he'd done something right today. Bruce was ten feet off the ground.

A few minutes later Ed strolled into the office.

" 'Morning, darlin' boy, suh," he said, heading for the coffeepot. "What's with Bruce? He's got a smile on his face a country mile long."

"I'm taking him with us when we go back to the hangar."

"Oh, you're at it again, tucking a spindly rooster under your wing. You did that in 'Nam and at Wright-Patterson when we were there. I think you have a father complex, Jace."

"What I have is a headache."

"Big night?"

"Lousy night. I upset Heather, then left her alone to calm down. Now I don't know if that was the right thing to do. Hell, I can't go on instinct like I do when I'm flying, because I've never been in love, so I don't have any instincts to go on!"

"Did that make sense?"

"Forget it," Jace said, staring moodily into his mug.

"Spill it, Jace. What did you do?"

"You know the slogan Buff pilots always use?"

" 'Ready, ready now.' Oh, cute. You didn't."

"I did. I opened my mouth and said it."

"Hell fire, Dalton! Why not invite her dead husband into the room with the two of you?"

"Dammit, I didn't think of it until it was too late!" Jace roared. "Oh-h-h, my head."

"Then you left her alone to stew on all that?"

"Well, yeah."

"Lord have mercy, boy! You're a dud! She slept with Wade's ghost instead of you. I swear, Jace, you need a training course in the courtship of skittish fillies. You are doing one hell of a lousy job!"

"Tell me about it," Jace said miserably.

"Now you're playing catch-up ball. Okay, tonight you are Mr. Wonderful. This calls for an extra dose of tender lovin' care."

"Yeah?"

"Hell, yes! A romantic dinner out, dancing, no heavy talk. Keep it light, get her to relax again. Sweet-talk her, Jace."

"Think so?"

"Know so. I can't believe how much you don't know about this. You've had more women over the years than—"

"I've never been in love before!" Jace bellowed.

"Excuse me, sirs," Bruce said, inching into the room. "The crew is here."

"Tell them to get started," Jace said gruffly. "They know what to do."

"Yes, sir," he said, saluting sharply. "Right away, sir."

"I'm not in a gung ho mood," Jace muttered as Bruce left the room.

Ed chuckled. "Finish your coffee. I'll go make sure everyone uses the right color crayon."

After Ed had left the office Jace squinted at the phone and toyed with the idea of calling Heather. It was still too early, he supposed, but he wanted to talk to her. Now!

He snatched up the receiver, slammed it back into place when he realized he didn't know her number, and reached for the telephone book.

Heather was lying in bed with the blankets pulled up to her chin. She'd been awake for an hour already, and it still wasn't time to get up. It had been a long night of tossing and turning and thinking about Jace Dalton. She had berated herself over and over for her behavior of the previous evening, and decided an apology was in order. Acting like a child was not the way to impress the man she was coming to care so deeply for. He had not intended to upset her, and her reaction had been ridiculous. Jace's use of the B-52 slogan was as normal as breathing to an Air Force man, and she'd responded as though he was the original ax murderer. And he'd been so sweet and kind when he'd asked her to come to the base. Oh, she was an idiot! A dunderhead! A—

The ringing of the telephone jolted her from her reverie, and she hurried into the living room to answer it.

"Hello?" she said.

"Heather? Jace. Did I wake you?"

"No, I was awake. Where are you?"

"At the base. Heather, look, about last night . . ."

"Oh, Jace, I'm so sorry."

"You are?" He frowned. "But—"

"I overreacted, and my behavior was immature and childish. I hope you'll accept my apology."

"Well, yeah, sure."

"Thank you."

"Would you like to go out to dinner tonight?"

"Oh, yes, that sounds lovely, Jace."

"Seven?"

"Perfect."

"I love you. Have a nice day at the agency."

"I will. Good luck with the X-82."

"Thanks, babe. See ya."

"Good-bye, Jace."

"I'll be damned," Jace said, slowly replacing the receiver. "I can't believe it. I'm not complaining, but I sure don't understand it."

When Jace walked into the room where the crew was busily at work, he smiled and gave Ed a thumb's up sign.

"Way to fly, Eagle Catcher," Ed said. "Just calls for a dose of Southern charm."

"Or whatever," Jace said. "I think I plain old lucked out."

"Don't quibble when you win. Just take your chips and run like hell."

"I intend to, Ace."

"You'll get the hang of this, mark my word."

"I'd better, major. There's a lot at stake here."

"Colonel, suh, you can't be beat by a little magnolia blossom. No suh, no way."

Jace grinned. "I hope you're right."

The crew appeared totally confused.

"You're not coloring, people!" Ed barked.

Jace laughed and shook his head. In the next instant he realized his headache had completely disappeared.

When Lori arrived at the agency Heather pounced. After asking if Lori was feeling well, then seating her behind her desk, Heather proceeded to pace the floor and talk for the next fifteen minutes straight.

Jace was in love with her, she said in a rush of words, and she was a breath away from falling in love with him. She told Lori about the various obstacles she saw standing in the way of her and Jace's future happiness, and about what had happened the previous night.

"Whew!" Lori said when Heather had finished and sat down. "My head is spinning. Oh, but, Heather, I'm so happy for you. Jace sounds absolutely wonderful."

"He is, but . . ."

"I know, I know, he's a pilot. But don't you see? Jace understands that you're frightened. He's only asking you to watch a takeoff and a landing, and I think that shows a great deal of sensitivity on his part. You need to go to that base on Monday, Heather."

"I realize that," she said, propping her elbows on the desk and cupping her chin in her hands.

"And?"

"And . . . I'll go."

"Good for you! Now, what are you going to wear for your special date tonight?"

"I don't know. I'll have to give it very careful consideration. Oh, Lori, I don't know if I want to be in love with Jace. This is not fun!"

"It'll get better. If you *are* in love with him, you can't push a button and turn it off. You've got to settle down and enjoy. Jace sounds like an extremely sexy man. Reap the rewards of said masculinity, my dear girl. Go to bed with the guy. It'll do wonders for your jangled nerves."

"Lori!"

"It will!"

"I'll think about it."

"No, don't think, just do it!"

"Lori, go take a nap. Mothers-to-be are supposed to get a lot of rest."

Lori laughed merrily, but Heather stared into space, frowning.

Jace Dalton was nervous. He looked in the mirror again, wondering if his charcoal gray suit was too somber, then glanced at his watch. He wasn't due at Heather's for another fifteen minutes, but the thought of waiting that long was not appealing.

He needed to see her, to hold her and kiss her. He just needed to know that everything was all right. She'd sounded fine on the phone that morning, but it wasn't the same as being with her. He was acting flaky, he thought. This was lady-killer Dalton? Hell, he was worse than a kid with his first crush. Bruce would perform better than this!

At least he was beginning to understand what Heather had said about losing oneself when in love. He'd been alone for years, but now he didn't feel complete unless he was with her. That wasn't good, but maybe it wasn't so terrible. There was nothing wrong with looking forward to being with the woman he loved. Yes, that made perfect sense. Love sure was complicated, though.

"Hell with it," he muttered. "I'm going over there now!"

Heather opened the door only a moment after he'd knocked on it. Beautiful, he thought immediately as she gestured him into the apartment. She was wearing a simply cut black cocktail dress, which bared her white shoulders and clung enticingly to her lovely body.

"Hello Jace," she said, her voice breathy.

"Heather." He cupped her face in his hands and looked down at her. "You're beautiful, so beautiful."

She met his warm blue gaze, and they shared a smile before he slowly lowered his head to hers. His mouth melted over hers in unhurried pleasure as he drank the sweetness from her lips, then parted them to seek her tongue. He pulled her closer, molding her to him as she responded to the kiss with total abandon. Her hands splayed over his back, and she relished his strength, the feel of his muscles bunching under her palms. As he swept his hands over her slender body, she pressed more tightly against him, savoring the feel of his mouth moving on hers.

"Heather," Jace murmured, his voice vibrant with desire, "I missed you."

"You what?" she asked bemusedly.

"I missed you. I suppose that's something like losing a part of myself because I love you. But, Heather, I like how it feels."

She stepped away from him. "I thought about that some more after we talked last night, Jace. I'm a woman now, not the child I was when I married Russ. I no longer fear losing my identity by loving someone."

"Then that's not a problem between us anymore?"

"No, not at all."

"So, now it's just my flying. No, dammit," he went on when she opened her mouth to speak, "don't even comment. We're not discussing any of that tonight. We're going to have a great time with no serious talk about anything that's distressing. Okay?"

"Very."

"Then we're off to do the town, my lady." He

pulled her back into his arms. "Oh, Heather, I love you so much."

Jace had made reservations at an exclusive restaurant that was nestled at the base of Camelback Mountain in Scottsdale. Ed had recommended it as being romantic as hell, with prices to match its vaunted reputation. They were seated at a small table in a dimly lit corner, and Heather said with a laugh that she could barely read the menu.

Jace didn't even bother to glance at it. He was too busy admiring Heather. Her dress had thin straps and a low, square neckline, and her bare skin looked like ivory velvet. He took one of her hands in his and smiled at her warmly.

"You're so lovely tonight, Heather," he said.

"Thank you. You look kind of gorgeous yourself. Jace, I want to tell you that I'll come to the base Monday morning. I know we weren't going to discuss anything heavy this evening, but I wanted you to know."

"Are you sure you want to?"

"I have to, Jace."

"It's a start, Heather. A good one."

"Yes, I know. I'll be fine. After all, you've assured me that you're a very good pilot."

"I am," he said, frowning slightly. There it was again, he thought. That emphasis on whether he was good at what he did. It meant something, but he didn't know what.

The food was delicious, the conversation lively. They drank a toast to each other, then clicked their glasses together once again in honor of Lori and

Jerry's baby. After coffee and dessert they went into the adjoining ballroom, where a small band was playing. As they danced a cloak of contentment settled over Heather. Jace's arms felt strong and protective. He rested his lips lightly on her forehead and cradled her hand close to his chest. The feel of his hard body brushing lightly against hers seemed to ignite a fire deep within her. Desire sparked between them, and the room, the other people all disappeared, and they were aware only of each other.

Jace's arms tightened about Heather and he buried his face in her soft, fragrant hair. "Heather," he said, his voice hoarse with passion, "let's get out of here."

"Yes," she whispered.

In the car Jace slid his hand to the back of her neck and pulled her to him to kiss her deeply.

"I want to make love to you, Heather," he said, his mouth close to hers.

"Yes, Jace. I want you too."

"I don't mean to rush you . . ."

"No, no, you're not. I've never been so sure of anything in my life. Let's go home, Colonel Dalton."

After another arousing kiss Jace turned the key in the ignition and the powerful car roared into action. As he drove he found it difficult to concentrate on the road. He'd never desired a woman as he did Heather, he thought. But then, he'd never loved anyone before, either. He had to cool off, take it slow and easy, so it would be perfect for her. He wanted her so damn much! He wanted to see, caress, kiss every inch of her silken body. Dammit, he thought as heat rose within him. He had to think about something else or he'd rush her and ruin everything. He'd think about the plane, the X-82. Oh, hell, he couldn't care less about that aircraft at the moment! He wanted to make love to Heather Wade!

"The stars are so pretty tonight," Heather said.

"What?" he yelled.

"Goodness, did I wake you?"

"Sorry," he mumbled. If Ed Turner could see him now, he'd laugh himself blue, Jace thought. Bed hoppin' Jace Dalton was coming apart at the seams! Heather was the Eagle Catcher, all right.

"Is something wrong, Jace?"

He chuckled. "No, nothing is wrong. I just love you a whole helluva lot, Heather."

She smiled, then leaned her head back with a quiet sigh of happiness. Her gaze flickered over Jace's magnificent body, and she felt the now welcome stirrings of desire deep within her. Tonight, she thought dreamily. This was the night when she and Jace would come together in the most intimate way. They would be one.

When they stepped out of the elevator on the fourth floor of their apartment building, Jace slipped his arm around Heather's shoulders and pulled her close.

"Your place or mine?" he whispered in her ear as they walked down the hall.

"Your place has a note taped to the door."

"Uh-oh." He yanked the paper from his door and quickly scanned it. "Dammit to hell!" he growled.

"What's wrong?"

"The base called the apartment manager. There's been a fire in the hangar housing the X-82. I've got to get out there right away!"

Six

The crackling sensual tension that had weaved around them was shattered by Jace's string of expletives. He unlocked his door and pulled Heather inside.

"Sit!" he said gruffly, then stalked into the bedroom and slammed the door behind him.

"Sit?" she said to the empty room. "Why not?" She threw up her hands and settled onto the sofa. "Do I get to roll over and play dead too?" Well, wasn't this just ducky! she thought. She had been about to embark upon a glorious night of lovemaking with that man, and his stupid plane catches on fire! Goodness, Jace was upset. She'd never heard some of these words he'd used. But what had caused his fury? Leaving her—or concern for the X-82? Oh, who was she kidding? It was the plane. The planes always came first with Air Force men. Always.

"Heather!" Jace roared, coming back into the room clad in jeans and an Air Force sweat shirt.

"Yes?"

He stopped in front of her, pulled her to her feet, and spoke, his mouth an inch from hers, his nose pressing against hers.

"I have never been so angry in my life!" he said through clenched teeth. "This was *our* night, yours and mine! What in the hell am I supposed to do if that damn plane melted into a lump of metal? Wave a magic wand and fix it? It doesn't take a colonel to put out a fire! Stay here, Heather. Right here! Don't move, because I'll be back as soon as I chew a few butts for pulling me out there when there is nothing I can do about the situation! Do not leave! Understand?"

Heather's head bobbed up and down, and there was a silly grin on her face. Jace kissed her roughly, then released her so abruptly that she toppled back onto the sofa. He slammed the door on his way out.

Heather struggled to sit up, then folded her hands primly in her lap. "It wasn't the plane that had him upset," she said happily, "it was leaving me! Me! There is smoke coming out of Jace Dalton's ears because he had to leave me!" She couldn't believe it! An Air Force pilot putting her before a plane? But that was what Jace had done, all right. Oh, heavens, it was wonderful, glorious, fantastic! She loved that man so much!

"What?" she whispered aloud, stunned by the thought.

It was true. The uncertainties were gone. The last niggling doubt had been whisked into oblivion. She was in love with Jace Dalton. She savored the realization, allowed it to bathe her in a euphoria. She wouldn't think about any of her fears now. When Jace returned she would tell him that she loved him.

She took off her shoes and curled up in the corner of the sofa. For the next hour she busied herself reading the magazines that were stacked on the coffee table. They were various military publications, and were boring at best. She yawned several times, walked around to keep herself awake, then settled back down, tucking a throw pillow under her head on the arm of the sofa. She'd close her eyes for a few minutes, she decided. Just for a few minutes.

The first streaks of dawn were inching across the sky when Jace pulled into the parking lot. His jaw was set in a tight, hard line as he bounded up the four flights of stairs two steps at a time, then strode down the hall to his apartment.

In his living room he stopped still and stared at the sleeping figure on his sofa. A gentle smile tugged at his lips. Heather was curled up in a ball, her head resting on a pillow on the arm of the sofa, her hand nestled near her cheek. Jace thought she was the loveliest sight he had ever seen. He stood looking at her for several more minutes, then got a blanket from the bedroom. He covered her with it, resisting the urge to kiss her slightly parted lips. With a sigh, he walked back into the bedroom, pulling off his sweat shirt as he headed for the shower.

The sound of water running brought Heather slowly out of her deep, dreamless sleep, and she sat up, blinking her eyes and wondering where she was. Her hand fell on the blanket, then her head snapped around in the direction of Jace's bedroom. Glancing at her watch, she saw it was nearly six A.M. She stood up, stretched, yawned, then walked into the bedroom. Just as she entered Jace emerged from the bathroom with a towel tucked low on his hips.

Their eyes met and held as neither moved, nor hardly breathed. Heather's heart was thundering as she tore her gaze from Jace's, and she drank in the sight of his splendid body. His chest was covered by damp, curly black hair that narrowed to a strip that disappeared below the towel. His shoulders, arms, legs were muscular, each in perfect proportion. His raven-dark wet hair was in tousled disarray, and when she met his gaze again, she saw desire reflected in the blue depths of his eyes.

"You are," she said breathlessly, "the most beautiful man I have ever seen."

Jace drew in his breath sharply, then stared at the ceiling for a moment as he strove for control. He ran his hand down his face, letting out a long rush of air.

"I'm so sorry, Heather," he said, his voice strained. "All I could think about while I was out there was you. I know you're hurt and angry because I had to leave you to go tend to a plane. It's probably reaffirmed in your mind that I'm in the Air Force and, therefore, you'll always take second seat to an airplane, but—"

"Jace, no! I know you didn't want to go. I know how angry you were because our time together was interrupted. I waited for you, Jace. I wouldn't have done that if I were blaming you for this. I—I love you. I truly love you so very much."

"Oh, Heather." He groaned, and pulled her into his arms, then lowered his head to claim her mouth.

The kiss was frenzied, as their tongues met and their passions soared. Jace pressed her to him, crushing her breasts against his chest with sweet pain. Heather melted into him, filling all of her senses with him, relishing the feel of his moist skin and steely muscles as she spread her hands like fans on his back.

"I want you," he murmured, his lips against hers. "Let me love you, Heather."

"Yes. Oh, yes, Jace."

With shaking hands, he pulled down the zipper at the back of her dress, then brushed the straps from her shoulders. The dress fell to the floor, and he shuddered slightly at the sight of her bare breasts. He cupped them, caressing the tender flesh, then lowered his head to flick his tongue over first one rosy nipple, then the other.

Heather clutched his shoulders, tipping her head back and closing her eyes to savor the potent sensations coursing through her. Jace drew a taut bud into his mouth, suckling it in a rhythmic motion that she felt in the secret darkness of her femininity.

"Oh, Jace," she whispered, swaying on her feet.

His breathing was labored as he looked at her. He slid his hands to her waist and slowly drew down her half slip and panty hose. Heather stepped away from the clothing, gasping when she saw the smoldering passion in Jace's eyes as he gazed at her nude body.

"You're so lovely," he said, his voice thick. "You're exquisite, Heather. And you're mine. You're mine."

He swept back the blankets on the bed, then extended his hand to her. She walked to his side, and he placed her on the cool sheets. When he dropped the towel to the floor, she held her breath, her gaze raking over his magnificent body. His manhood boldly announced his need and desire for her. She lifted her arms to welcome him into her embrace, and he stretched out next to her, pulling her close and burying his face in the lush fullness of her breasts. His hand rested on the smooth plane of her stomach as he raised his head to claim her mouth, his tongue plunging deep within.

Her fingers sank into his thick hair, urging him closer as ecstasy swirled through her. Jace tore his mouth from hers and drew a ragged breath, then, using his lips and tongue, his teeth and hands, he learned all the secrets of her soft body. Wherever he touched her he ignited a flame of passion.

"Jace!" she gasped when his hand slid to the inner warmth of her thigh.

"Soon, Heather, soon," he promised, his voice hoarse.

Desire ripped through him, but still he held back, his muscles trembling from the effort. The sensual pleasure of seeing Heather, of touching her, was intoxicating, and he ached to know her completely. Passion burned within him, and a moan rumbled up from his chest as his hand found the heated warmth of her femininity.

"Oh, please!" she cried.

"Yes!"

He moved over her, parting her legs with his knee, then hesitated as he gazed down at her flushed face.

"I love you, Jace," she whispered.

With a throaty groan, he entered her willing body, burying himself deep within her honeyed warmth. And then he began to move. With steady, powerful strokes, he lifted her away from reality. He slid his arm under her hips to bring her closer yet, to fill her, to consume her. Heather arched her back, meeting his thrusts as she clung to his shoulders.

Higher they soared. Their heartbeats thundered as they moved faster. Faster and harder, like waves pounding against the shore.

"Jace!" she gasped.

"Yes! Now, Heather! Now!"

Ecstasy swept through her body, carrying her away to a magical place. She heard Jace call her name as, with one final thrust, he joined her there. Sated, he collapsed against her, then kissed her tenderly, lovingly. When he lifted his head he gazed down at her, his blue eyes warm and gentle.

"I don't know what to say to you," he said, his voice husky. "I love you, Heather. There just aren't words to express how I feel."

"And I love you, Jace," she said, cradling his face in her hands. "I've never experienced anything so beautiful and . . . I love you so much."

He kissed her once more, then moved away, tucking her close to his side, their heads resting on the same pillow.

"You must be exhausted," she said. "You've been up all night."

"Mmmm."

"Are you already asleep?" she asked, smiling at him.

"Mmmm," he said, his dark lashes fanned against his cheeks.

Heather laughed softly and pulled the blankets up over them. Within a few minutes Jace's deep, steady breathing told her he was asleep, and she rested her hand lightly on his chest to feel the beating of his heart. A delicious languor settled over her, along with a rush of infinite joy.

Oh, how she loved this man, she thought dreamily. Their lovemaking had been beyond description in its beauty and splendor. She snuggled closer to him and there, held safely in his arms, she slept.

They woke around noon. Heather put her black cocktail dress back on, feeling a little silly wearing it in the middle of the day, and returned to her apartment. While she showered and changed, Jace would make lunch.

Her breasts were tender as the warm water beat against them, and there was a delicious soreness in various locations of her body. She savored each sensation, replaying in her mind the lovemaking she had shared with Jace. She was aglow with happiness, and hurried to dress in corduroys and a blouse so she could return to him.

When he opened his door in answer to her knock he swept her into his arms and kissed her passionately.

"Heavens," she said breathlessly.

"These self-locking doors are terrific," he said, grinning. "They lend themselves to great greetings."

Lunch consisted of huge sandwiches Jace had concocted from a vast array of ingredients. He ate two to her one, and declared himself to be a fantastic cook as he hadn't burned a thing. When Heather pointed out that he hadn't used the stove to prepare the meal, he said it was a mere technicality. They laughed and talked, and had a tendency to lose track of what they were saying as they gazed into each other's eyes. Finally, over coffee,

Heather asked Jace what had happened at the base earlier.

"What a zoo," he said, shaking his head. "Some wiring short-circuited in the ceiling of the hangar and started a fire. It was more smoke than anything, but they came barreling in there, drenching the place with water."

"Is the X-82 all right?"

"Yeah, it just got a bath, that's all. They murdered the computer, the cards, and the simulator. Can you believe that? Those guys went crazy with the hoses. I had to get on the phone to Edwards Air Force Base and tell them to fly the backup simulator over here, plus a new computer and system cards. Then, of course, someone wrote up a nifty press release stating that all was well, and would proceed on schedule. Hell. They wanted me to stick around while they moved the X-82 to a new hangar, but I said no way. They can tow a jet a few hundred yards without me. Luckily, I had all the test printouts in my office, or they'd have drowned those too."

"Will you have to go back out today?"

"Nope. I left instructions to put the stuff from Edwards in the hangar and said I'd be back Monday morning. Now, should the general call and tell me to haul my butt out there, I will reconsider my stand on the issue."

"I should hope so."

He chuckled. "Man, I was hot. I was barking orders like a Marine, and everyone was keeping out of my way. All except my buddy Ed, of course. He just stood there laughing his fool head off, telling me I did a great impression of a fire-breathing dragon. But, hell, I wanted to be with you, not with a bunch of hose-happy airheads."

"Goodness, you're fierce."

"Damn right," he said smugly. "I'm a mean, lean, tough dude. Except around generals. Then I'm politeness personified, a paragon of patience, a—"

"Stow it."

"Right."

At that moment the phone rang.

"Uh-oh," Jace said.

"Do you think it's the base?" Heather asked.

"Probably, but I sure as hell hope not," he said, striding into the living room. " 'Lo?" he said after snatching up the receiver.

"Howdy, darlin' boy, suh," Ed said. "How's life?"

"Fantastic, until five seconds ago. What do you want, corn pone?"

"Well, the general has a bee in his bonnet about you being here to supervise setting up the new equipment from Edwards. No one touches nothin' until Colonel Dalton, suh, is on the scene. I offered to take charge, but he said no dice."

"Hell."

"Sorry, Jace. I tried."

"Yeah, well, thanks anyway. I'll be out there in a while."

"How's that pretty little Eagle Catcher of yours?"

"Absolutely beautiful."

"Ain't love somethin'? It's as sweet as magnolia pie."

"They don't make a pie out of magnolias."

"This Southern boy does. See ya soon, darlin' boy, suh."

"Yeah," Jace said, chuckling as he hung up the phone.

"Jace?" Heather said, coming up behind him.

"Well," he said, turning to face her, "I have to supervise the setting up of the new equipment. Say, are you playing hooky from the travel agency today?"

"No, Lori and I take turns working Saturdays. I'm free."

"Damn, and I'm not. There are times when generals really get on my nerves."

Jace gathered her against his chest, one hand woven through her silky curls, the other on her back. She circled his waist with her arms and leaned into his warmth and strength. They simply stood there, not speaking, holding on to the one they loved.

"I . . ." Jace began, then cleared his throat roughly. "It's getting late."

"Yes. They'll be wondering what happened to you."

The kiss they shared left her trembling, then Heather was alone. With dragging steps she left Jace's apartment and returned to her own.

It was after eight that night when Heather opened her door to a frowning Jace Dalton.

"Remember me?" he asked, coming into the

apartment and pulling her into his arms. "Or am I just a blurry memory from your past?"

"You look vaguely familiar," she said, smiling up at him. "Kiss me and see if it jogs my brain."

The kiss was powerful and demanding, and Heather wrapped her arms around his neck as his tongue sought and found hers. His hands roamed over her back, then down the gentle slope of her hips, cradling her to him. Desire swirled through her, and she pressed her body eagerly against his.

"Yes," she said breathlessly when he finally released her, "I definitely know who you are. You've had a long day."

"No joke."

"Would you like some dinner?"

"No, they brought sandwiches in." He led her to the sofa and pulled her down beside him.

"So, what happened?"

"Heather," he said, raking a restless hand through his hair, "I need to explain something to you. Computers have made a tremendous difference in reducing the risk factor for test pilots. The majority of problems can be worked out before the plane ever leaves the ground, through hundreds of hours spent on the simulator. But sometimes . . . well . . ."

"Jace, what are you telling me?"

"Everyone was at the base, the general, the entire crew of the X-82. After the new equipment was set up the general called a meeting to get an update on the progress we were making. The computer printouts continually indicated that the

X-82 won't lift off the runway, yet there's no plausible reason why it shouldn't. Machines can only do so much. At some point the human element has to be brought into play. The general felt that the time had come for actual hands-on testing, and I thoroughly agreed with him."

"You flew it?" she whispered. "You flew the X-82?"

"I had to! We were at a dead end with the simulator. I've seen this happen before. The pilot has to step in and take over."

"Oh, God, Jace!"

"Listen to me," he said, gripping her by the shoulders. "All I did was take the plane up, circle the field, and land it. Some of the gauges were off just enough to screw up the computer, but once I figured that out, it went as smooth as glass. There's nothing defective about that airplane."

"But you could have been killed! All these hours I've been sitting here waiting for you, you could have been dead, and I wouldn't even have known or—"

"Heather, no! I'm telling you that it wasn't that risky, and you've got to believe me. Every major problem had been eliminated, so we knew it had to be something simple, and it was."

"Oh, Jace," she said, shaking her head.

"I promised you I'd tell you everything I was doing, and I'm keeping my word. I'm here. I'm alive. Nothing went wrong. Would you have preferred that I lie to you? I could have made up a story about why I was gone so long. We must have a relationship based on honesty, trust, Heather. Do you understand?"

Heather swallowed past the lump in her throat, and tried desperately to sort through the jumble in her mind. No, she wouldn't want Jace to lie to her, to treat her like a child who needed protection from reality. The X-82 was a hazy blur, an unknown entity she had never seen. Maybe after she saw Jace in the other jet on Monday it would all fall into place, become more real. She would watch him take off and land, which was no more than he had done in the X-82. She'd put it all on mental hold for now, and pray she'd find her inner peace on Monday morning.

"Heather?"

She took a trembling breath. "Thank you for telling me, Jace," she said.

"Are you okay?"

"Yes. Really, I am."

"Oh, Heather." He cradled her face in his hands. "It's all coming together for us, don't you see?"

"I . . . hope so."

"Tell me again that you're okay."

"I'm fine!" she said, smiling at him.

"You sure look fine," he said, trailing a ribbon of kisses down her throat. "And smell fine, and taste fine . . ."

"All that?"

"Yep. Whew! What you do to me is lethal. Stop kissing me."

"Right. Jace, would you like to drive up to Canyon Lake tomorrow? It would be a nice outing, and a chance to forget all this for a few hours. I could pack a picnic basket."

"I can't, Heather. The general wants us to resume the simulator tests in the morning and try to make up some of the time we've lost."

"Oh, Jace, really? One day is going to make that much difference?"

"He thinks so, I guess. I'm sorry. I'd rather spend the day with you. I hope you know that."

"Yes, of course I do," she said, forcing a weak smile.

"Hey, don't." He traced his finger over her cheek. "You look so sad. A lot of people have to work overtime. It has nothing to do with it being the Air Force. Things come up, and people put in extra hours. It's a common occurrence."

"Particularly in the military," she said, unable to keep the petulance out of her voice.

"Don't judge the military so harshly, Heather," he said, a sudden sharpness in his own voice. "I know it doesn't hold fond memories for you, but you have to be fair about it."

"Well, excuse me, colonel," she said tightly. "I'll consider myself scolded and sent to my room. Would you like me to salute first?"

"Oh, hell," he said, raking his hand through his hair. "Heather, I'm beat. I've had a brutal day, and I don't want to get in a hassle with you. Let's just drop it, okay? Enough is enough."

"Don't you get tired of them controlling your life? That general will be home with his family tomorrow while you're working yourself to death. And it won't be him who risks his life flying the X-82. It'll be you!"

"Because that's what I do for a living!" Jace said none too quietly, pushing himself to his feet. "When are you going to accept that?"

"Never!" she cried, her voice shrill. "I hate those planes! I wasn't even going to think about this again until Monday, but there's no getting away from it! What's in it for me, except the waiting and the prayer they don't come knocking on my door and tell me you're dead!"

"Dammit, Heather, how many times do I have to say this? I'm a good pilot, and I don't take any unnecessary risks! I didn't today, and I won't in the future. I—Oh, hell, I've had enough of this. I need some sleep."

Jace spun on his heel and stalked to the door as Heather stumbled to her feet. Before she could speak, he had left the apartment, slamming the door behind him.

"Oh, no," she whispered. "Oh, Jace, no!"

What had she done? She'd lashed out at Jace like a shrew, acting as though it were his fault he had to work tomorrow. He hadn't volunteered, not the way Russ always had. Then she'd ranted on about the planes. Granted, she'd had a long, miserable day waiting for Jace to come home, but he hadn't chosen to stay away. He'd looked so exhausted, and there she'd sat, screaming her head off. She had to go apologize.

"No," she said aloud, "he said he needed to get some sleep. I'll just make it worse if I wake him.

Oh, me and my big mouth! I wanted to make love with that man, not war!"

In his own apartment Jace poured himself a glass of milk and downed it in three swallows. He slammed the glass onto the counter, and the force of the impact caused the glass to shatte., cutting the palm of his right hand.

"Dammit to hell!" he roared, turning on the cold water and shoving his hand under the icy stream. "Ouch! Damn it! Ouch!" Wonderful, he thought fiercely. The perfect cap for a helluva day. Well, it hadn't been all bad. The X-82 had finally flown and . . . Heather. Maybe he should have called her at some point and let her know he was in for a long siege at the base. She'd been cooped up all day because she hadn't known when he'd get back, then he'd come in and announced he had to work tomorrow. And did he really expect her to be over her fear of planes just because he'd had a nice jaunt in the X-82? No, wounds didn't heal that quickly.

"You blew it again, Dalton," he said. "You jumped all over her. It's not her fault you're tired and—Lord, I'm bleeding to death here!"

Jace yanked his hand from the water and pressed a towel to it. A few moments later he peered at the cut and grimaced. The blood was still flowing freely.

"I need stitches," he muttered. "Why me? All I want to do is make love to my lady, then get some sleep!" He was not, he decided firmly, going all the way back to the base to get this thing tended to.

He'd pay whatever it cost, as long as the medical facility was close by. So, how was he going to drive? Well, this was one way to get back into Heather's apartment. Bleed all over her floor!

When the knock sounded at the door Heather hurried to answer it.

"Hi," Jace said brightly. "Could we declare a truce for a while? I have a small problem."

"What kind of—Jace, your hand! There's blood on that towel."

"That's the small problem."

"Come in here."

"No, what I need is for you to come out and drive me to an emergency room. Would you mind?"

"How badly are you hurt?" she said, her eyes wide.

"I just need a couple of stitches. Heather, I'm really sorry I hollered at you about—"

"Forget that," she said, grabbing her purse. "You have to get medical attention before you faint from loss of blood!"

"Well, that's stretching it a bit, but—"

"Come on," she said, pulling the door closed. "Do you feel dizzy? Can you walk?"

He grinned. "Are you planning on carrying me?"

"Jace! Get serious! That towel is soaked with blood. Move!"

"Yes, ma'am," he said, striding after her as she ran down the hall and punched the button for the elevator.

In the elevator Jace nearly choked on his suppressed laughter as Heather pushed him against the wall and planted her hands on his chest.

"I'm not going to pass out," he said.

"You never know. I've got to keep you on your feet, because if you fell down I wouldn't be able to lift you."

"Heather, if I go over, you won't be capable of stopping me."

"You're dizzy?" she shrieked.

"No! I was simply stating a fact. Never mind. Don't you know you're supposed to kiss the walking wounded?"

"Hush," she said as the elevator doors swished open. "Do you want to wait in the lobby while I get my car?"

"No, of course not."

"You don't have to do a macho number for me, Jace."

"I can walk to the car, Heather," he growled.

"Well, don't blame me if you get a concussion when you land on the pavement."

"Oh, man!" he said, rolling his eyes.

Heather glared at Jace, then hurried across the parking lot to her car. She opened the door for him, and he attempted to hide his smile as he bent his head and slid onto the seat.

"Aaagh," he moaned.

"What's wrong?" Heather yelled. "Are you in pain?"

"I can't fold up in here! My knees are in my mouth! My head is hitting the top of—"

"Oh, is that all?" she said, slamming the door and running around to the driver's side.

"Heather, I'm a pretzel!"

"Jace, be quiet! The important thing here is your hand. Keep that towel wrapped tightly around it. Put your head down if you feel dizzy."

"I can't move!"

"Then you won't fall over, will you?" she said as she headed for the exit.

Jace looked over at her, a gentle smile tugging at his lips. How he loved her, he thought. They'd had a wingding of an argument, and now here she was, driving him to the hospital because he needed help. She'd taken control of the situation with a no-nonsense attitude, crammed him into her car, and off they went. She was a lot tougher than she gave herself credit for. With her inner strength, she could overcome her fear of planes. She just didn't realize it yet. She was still in the initial stage of fright, but she could beat it. She could! And he would help her with patience and understanding . . . and with tender loving. Lots of tender loving, sweet as magnolia pie.

"I love you, Heather," he said quietly.

"Oh, Jace, I love you too," she said, glancing at him. "I'm sorry I was so unreasonable before. I know you didn't volunteer to work tomorrow. I was acting like a child who didn't get her own way. I really am sorry."

"Well, I pushed you about accepting the fact that I fly planes for a living. I know you need more time to adjust. And I should have called you today and told you I was going to be so late. I'm sorry."

She sighed. "There seem to be so many obstacles in our path, and I'm the one who's put them there. It's *my* fears that are building the wall that's keeping us from—"

"Heather, no, don't say that. We're going to work all of this out, you'll see. We love each other. We can overcome anything standing in our way because we have that love."

"Can we, Jace?" she said softly.

"Yes! We'll—"

"Here's the hospital. Let's just concentrate on getting your hand fixed. Unfold your pretzel body."

Inside the emergency room Jace answered questions for the necessary forms. His signature was an illegible scrawl, due to the thick towel wrapped around his hand. He was whisked away by a shapely blond nurse who smiled at him ever so sweetly. Heather sent murderous mental messages to the woman, then settled onto a chair in the waiting room.

What a crazy day, she thought, shaking her head. She'd shared exquisite lovemaking with Jace, been dumped back in her apartment for an endless stretch of hours, had a screamer with said lover, and was now playing the heroine by keeping the last drop of his life's blood from dripping from his body. And through it all she'd loved him.

When Jace returned, his hand bandaged, he appeared rather pale.

"Are you all right?" Heather asked, hurrying to catch up as he strode out the door.

"You should have seen the size of the needle they jammed into my hand! It was enormous! I've got five stitches in this dumb thing. How can I fly the simulator with five stitches in my hand, for Pete's sake? And furthermore, *I'm* driving us home!"

"You are not!"

"Heather, I refuse to stuff my knees in my mouth again! I can put the seat back if I drive."

"But your hand . . ."

"It's numb! Dead! It could fall off and I'd never know it. Give me the keys."

Heather handed him the keys, then burst into laughter. "You're the lousiest patient I've ever seen," she said. "How did you cut yourself in the first place?"

"I don't wish to discuss it," he said stiffly, causing her laughter to erupt again.

During the drive back to the apartment building Jace grumbled about the traffic, the size of his bandage, and the huge bill he'd paid at the hospital in exchange for a few less than fancy stitches. Heather looked out the side window to conceal the smile she was unable to keep from creeping onto her lips.

When they stepped out of the elevator on the fourth floor Jace strode down the hall, then stopped abruptly in front of his door.

"Would you like to come in for . . . um, a drink?" he asked.

"Well, yes, that sounds nice," she said, "but I thought you wanted to go to bed. I mean, you said you needed to get some sleep."

"Come in," he said gruffly, inserting the key in the lock. He pushed the door open, then stepped back for her to enter.

In the living room he turned on the lights and the stereo, turned the stereo off again, then ran his uninjured hand through his hair.

"Heather," he said, spinning around to face her, "I—Don't you want to sit down?"

"Thank you," she said, and sat on the sofa.

"Now then," he said, clearing his throat, "I think we need to talk about this, so there won't be any misunderstandings."

"Talk about what?"

"Sex."

"What?" she said, her eyes widening.

"Sex, per se. In our case, it's making love, and there's a helluva big difference between the two. Anyway, I don't want to appear that I'm taking you for granted, but by the same token, when people are in love, how much discussion is necessary about whether or not they intend to . . . Is this coming across as rather clinical?"

"You're doing fine, Jace. Carry on. You were saying?"

"Yes, well, the way I see it, we should be together as much as possible."

"Meaning?"

"Make love at night and wake up in the same bed in the morning, dammit! I don't want to pull on my clothes and sneak out of your place or vice versa. I love you, Heather, and I want you next to me through the whole damn night. Understand?"

"Why are you yelling?"

"I have no idea," he said, shaking his head. "I think I'm slipping over the edge."

"You're exhausted, poor darling," she said, getting up and circling his waist with her arms. "You really should go to bed. Would you like me to tuck you in?"

"Weren't you listening to a word I said?" he bellowed.

"I certainly was, colonel, sir," she said, unbuttoning her shirt and dropping it on the floor. "Everything came across loud and clear," she continued. Her bra followed her shirt, then she kicked off her shoes and pushed corduroys and panties down her legs.

Jace blinked once slowly, then drew an unsteady breath as his gaze raked over her naked form. He felt his manhood swell as he drank in her loveliness.

"You are an incredible woman, Heather Wade," he said, his voice husky with desire. "You've brought so much joy to my life. You're so beautiful, and warm, and loving. I probably don't deserve you, but I'm going to hold fast to your love, Heather, for the rest of my life. You're mine."

"Yes," she whispered. "Yes, I am. Make love to me, Jace. Take me to the special place I can only journey to with you. I want to be with you now, and wake up next to you in the morning."

With a throaty moan, he pulled her into his arms and kissed her deeply, his tongue delving into her mouth as his hands roamed over her silky skin. Then he swung her into his arms and carried her to the bedroom. He set her down and quickly shed his clothing as he threw back the blankets on the bed.

They reached for each other with an urgency that engulfed them both, then they came together with a vehemence that took their breath away. Their lovemaking was frenzied, wild, as they soared above reality. Their hearts were pounding, their breathing labored, as they exploded into ecstasy. They clung to each other, lingering in that treasured place, then they drifted slowly back to the real world.

"Oh, Heather," Jace said, moving gently away. "I love you so much."

"And I'm glad," she said, curling up next to him, "because I love you too."

"I'll try not to wake you when I leave in the morning."

"Will you be gone all day?"

"I don't know for sure. It depends on how it goes."

"All right."

"This has been quite a day, hasn't it?" He chuckled. "A little bit of everything. Even the X-82 did its act. Good night, Heather."

"Good night, Jace."

Jace was asleep within minutes, but Heather lay by his side, wide awake. His final words pressed like a heavy weight on her heart and mind. The planes. They were there, never far from their existence, in every shape and size, and they frightened her to the very recesses of her soul.

Seven

The first thought Heather had when she awoke the next morning was that she no longer detested the start of a new day. Mornings were glorious, wonderful, fantastic, when they included Jace Dalton.

She had slept through the sounds of his shower and dressing, but stirred when several mumbled expletives inched into her consciousness. Jace was sitting in a chair, his head bent.

"Hi," she said, stretching leisurely. "What are you grumbling about?"

"I can't tie my shoes. My damn hand is stiff and swollen."

"Say no more," she said, throwing back the blankets. "Heather Wade to the rescue."

Jace's head snapped up, and his intake of breath was so sharp it was actually painful, as Heather walked, naked, across the room. She dropped to her knees in front of him, tied his shoes, patted each bow, then lifted her gaze to his. Their eyes locked together, speaking of love . . . then of desire.

Jace's hands were trembling slightly as he filled them with her breasts, his thumbs trailing over the nipples, bringing each to a taut bud. Neither spoke as he slid his hands to her waist, lifting her up and settling her onto his lap. His fingers trailed a heated path over the flat plane of her stomach, down the outer slope of her leg, then back up to the inner warmth of her thigh. His breath quickened, as did hers, and she wrapped her arms around his neck and buried her face in his throat.

"Heather," Jace said, his voice harsh with passion.

"Oh, Jace." She heard the tremor in her own voice. "I want you. Oh, how I want you."

With a throaty moan, he lifted her to her feet, then stood, drawing a deep, shuddering breath as he strove for control. His manhood was straining against the confines of his slacks. He was aching with the need to consume her, to bury himself in her.

"I've got to get to the base," he said, his voice strained as he turned to look at her.

"Oh, of course, I'm sorry," she said, crossing her arms over her breasts. "I guess I'll go back to sleep for a while. You . . . um, have a nice day." She moved around him and walked toward the bed.

"Oh, the hell with it!" he said, striding after her.

He spun her around and brought his mouth down hard on hers.

With a sound that was a combination of a purr and a moan, Heather flung her arms around his neck and answered the demands of his lips and tongue. The buckle of his belt dug into her soft flesh, though, and she stiffened.

"I'm hurting you," Jace said hoarsely. "This belt has got to go."

Heather helped him remove his clothing and shoes, then scrambled back onto the bed. Jace's naked body was soon covering hers. The heat from his body kindled the embers of desire within her to a raging flame, and she burrowed her fingers into his hair and pulled his head down to hers. His tongue plummeted deep into her mouth as he parted her thighs and entered her with a bold thrust that seemed to draw the breath from her body. The raging rhythm of their union carried them away until the rocketing spasms came at journey's end.

Jace collapsed against her, then pushed himself up to gaze at her flushed face. They shared a warm smile, then he moved away, propping himself up on his elbow and resting his head in his hand.

"That," he said with a chuckle, "is what is known as a quickie."

"It was delightful," she said, trailing her finger through the moist curls on his chest. "Pretty nice payment, when all I did was tie your shoes. What do I get for buttoning your shirt or zipping your pants?"

He laughed, then swung off the bed. Heather's gaze traced over the smooth muscles of his back, his tight buttocks and powerful legs.

She sighed. "You are so gorgeous, Dalton."

"Oh, yeah? I'm glad you approve, because I'm all yours. I'm also late. Another quick shower and I'm gone."

A short time later he was showered and redressed in his uniform. He propped his feet one at a time on the bed for Heather to tie his shoes, telling her firmly to keep her luscious body covered while she performed the task. After one more searing kiss, he left the apartment. Heather snuggled down under the blankets and drifted off into a contented slumber.

It was after ten when she woke again. She returned to her apartment, and after showering, dressing, and drinking two cups of coffee, she snatched up her purse and headed out the door. Her destination was her parents' home, her mission to water the plants.

She drove along Indian School Road, then turned onto Scottsdale Road. Leaving the main thoroughfare a mile later, she wove her way through an attractive subdivision that boasted a multitude of orange and grapefruit trees. Her parents lived in a three-bedroom ranch-style house surrounded by fruit trees.

Heather let herself in the front door, watered the vast variety of plants, which were her mother's pride and joy, then sank onto the sofa. She felt different, she thought, as though she were a stranger sitting in that room. And, in a way, it was true. She had been little more than a child when she had bid her parents good-bye as they left for their cruise, and now she was a woman. A woman in love.

Tomorrow, she thought. Tomorrow she would watch Jace fly in a silver jet. The engines would burst alive, scream across the desert, then lift the metal coffin off the ground and out of view.

"Oh, Jace," she murmured, pressing her fingertips to her temples, "why can't I be stronger, have more courage? You deserve better than this, but I'm so frightened. So terribly frightened." No, darn it, she was not going to spend the day in a state of depression. She was going to . . . buy a new dress! Yes, that was a great idea. A real knock-out of a dress that would shoot Jace's temperature up a notch or two. What a delicious thought. Not that Colonel Dalton needed much encouragement to make mad, passionate love to her. "You're naughty, Heather," she said merrily as she left the house, her buoyant mood restored.

When Jace arrived at his office Bruce told him that the general wanted to see him at once, and that the general's aide was waiting outside to drive him across the base. Jace spun on his heel and stalked out, yelling over his shoulder to Bruce that the crew was to do nothing until he returned. Jace then asked the heavens why, *why* had the general requested his presence on the one day he had been late reporting for duty? But, he decided an instant later, the lovemaking he had shared with Heather was well worth any reprimand he might receive regarding his tardiness.

The meeting consisted of nothing more than a discussion of another press release regarding the X-82, and Jace left the general's office a short time later. He refused the offer from the aide for a ride back, deciding to walk instead. As he strolled leisurely his mind skittered once more to Heather, to their lovemaking.

She was both an innocent child and a sensuous woman. When they had made love she had gazed at him with an expression of love and trust. No bigger than a whisper, she held the power to crush him into dust, take the sunshine from his life, sentence him to a world of loneliness.

For the first time in Jace Dalton's adult life, he was vulnerable, and he swung back and forth on an emotional pendulum between euphoria and chilling fear. During his career he had viewed each new aircraft to which he had been assigned as an exciting challenge. He never doubted for a moment that he would conquer the metal monster, bring it under his control, then demand and receive the finest performance within its capabilities. He flew with skill and confidence, and was respected by his peers and viewed with awe by the young airmen just starting out.

But now he was dealing with something completely unknown. Love. None of his experiences had prepared him for the complexities of this powerful emotion. He was not in command at all, and was susceptible to love's whims, the highs and lows it dealt him. It was heaven in the form of Heather's smile, her laughter, the lovemaking they shared. And it was hell when she cried, and when he realized he could lose her to the fears within her.

Love was an equalizer, declaring him to be nothing more than a man, stripped bare of power, rank, control. He had nothing to offer Heather but his heart, mind, body, and soul. He could only give himself, and pray that it was enough.

Four jets screamed high above Jace in the clear blue sky, and he stopped, turning to watch as they flew nearly as one in synchronized beauty, then disappeared in the distance.

The planes, he thought, resuming his walk. They were a part of him. His world had centered on flying for as long as he could remember. He performed his other duties as a colonel to achieve the ultimate goal: hours spent flying miles above the ground, free, away from the turmoil below. But now there was Heather, and his world encompassed her too. It was as though there were two of him—Colonel Dalton, the pilot, and Jace Dalton, the man. He didn't want to be torn apart, forced to choose between Heather and the planes. He wanted, no, he *needed* both to be complete, whole within himself, he thought as he pulled open the door and entered his office.

A few minutes later he was on his way to the hangar, where he ran into Ed Turner.

"What happened to your hand?" Ed asked.

"Nice, huh? I broke a glass," Jace said. "The damn thing is going to be a real nuisance."

"You got stitches in that hand or what?"

"Five stitches."

"How are you going to handle the stick in the simulator?"

"I don't know yet. I may have to watch over your shoulder for a few days. You're the backup pilot on this, so our test hours have to be equal anyway. I can catch up later."

"Whatever. Being backup behind you, darlin' boy, means my butt stays on the ground. You check 'em, you fix 'em, you fly 'em."

Jace laughed. "That's right, buddy, but you've got to be ready to step in just in case."

"In case of what? Hell freezing over? That's what it would take to keep you on the ground, Jace."

The series of tests went smoothly, and morale was high. Jace dismissed the crew at two o'clock, telling them not to report until ten the next morning, as he had his proficiency flying to do. Then he and Ed went to the officers' club for lunch.

"The simulator handled sweet," Ed said as they ate steak sandwiches and double orders of fries.

"I could tell," Jace said. "I'm itching to get my hands on that honey again, but I'll obviously have to wait until this embroidery work is gone. Ed, you're looking after Heather tomorrow morning, remember?"

"Jace, how can you fly a T-38 if you can't work the stick on the X-82?"

"It's not that long a flight compared to the hours

we put in today. I'll pack my hand with gauze and tape it really tight."

"Why not just postpone?"

"No, I don't want to do that. Heather has agreed to come watch, and it's got to go as scheduled. It's important."

"You're a stubborn Yankee, ya know that?"

"Eat your lunch, corn pone. I realize steak isn't as tempting as magnolia pie, but it will have to do."

"Your pretty little Eagle Catcher sounds like a fine, fine lady, Jace. I'm happy for you."

"Thanks, Ed. I just hope that I don't . . . Well, never mind."

"Don't what?"

"Lose her," Jace said quietly. "Her fear of the planes is real, it's big, and it's as threatening as hell to what we have together. The thought of her walking away from me causes an ache in my gut. She's a part of me, an extension of who I am."

"So is flying, Jace. So are the planes."

"I know, I know. I'm going home, Ed. I've seen enough of this place for one day."

"You haven't finished your lunch."

"I guess I'm not as hungry as I thought I was." Jace stood up. "See you in the morning, Ace."

"Yeah, okay. And, Jace? Give Heather some more time to adjust. Everything is going to work out just fine."

"I sure as hell hope so. 'Bye."

"See ya, Eagle Catcher," Ed said, a deep frown on his face.

*　　*　　*

When Jace got home he went directly to Heather's apartment and knocked on the door. When there was no answer he entered his own apartment, calling to her as he shut the door behind him. The silence that greeted him made his dark brows knit together. He hadn't noticed whether her car was in the parking lot. He'd simply figured she was waiting for him. A flash of irritation swept through him as he realized that Heather wasn't there, but in the next instant he knew he was unjustified in assuming she would wait around for him when he had given no indication as to when he would return.

He changed from his uniform to jeans and a white sweater. then sank onto the sofa, drumming his fingers on the end table. Where in the hell was she? he wondered. No, she wasn't accountable to him. She was an independent woman with a mind of her own. But where in the hell was she?

Mentally throwing up his hands at his irrational thoughts, Jace flicked on the television. A few minutes later he turned it off again, opened the apartment door, and peered out into the hall. On impulse, he strode down to Heather's apartment and knocked, figuring she could have come home but not stopped to check if he was back.

"Damn," he said when there was no answer.

An hour later Jace was not a happy man. He had finally propped his door open halfway so he could see Heather when she came down the hall, then proceeded to pace the floor of his living room. The question of where Heather could be produced a wide variety of answers. She'd gone to the movies, the library, the grocery store. She'd had car trouble. No, worse than that. She'd been in an accident! She's been mugged! Were there muggers in Phoenix? She was partying it up with a bunch of her friends in some sleazy bar. He'd wring her neck! How would he know if she'd been in an accident? She could be lying unconscious in a hospital and—

A movement out in the hall caught his eye and he flung the door open.

"Jace!" Heather gasped. "Goodness, you startled me."

"Where in the hell have you been?" he bellowed, planting his hands on his hips. Uh-oh, he thought an instant later. He was definitely in trouble.

The expressions on Heather's face changed in rapid succession from surprise to confusion to rip-roaring anger. She squinted at him, pursed her lips together, then tilted her nose in the air and stomped down the hall.

"Oh, hell," Jace said, hurrying after her. "Heather, wait!"

She inserted her key in the door and entered her apartment with Jace close on her heels. Placing her purse and packages on the sofa, she went into the kitchen and took a bottle of soda from the refrigerator.

"Heather," Jace said, when she returned to the living room. "I was worried about you, that's all. I shouldn't have yelled, but I didn't know where you were and, well, I missed you. I want to be with you every minute possible, which isn't realistic because you have your own life to lead, but whoever said that men in love were rational creatures? Right? I'm sorry I hollered, but I'm very glad you're home. I really did miss you, Heather."

A silence hung over the room as Jace stared at Heather. He couldn't read the expression on her face. The seconds ticked by, and he felt a trickle of perspiration run down his back.

"I think," she said finally, setting the soda on the end table and taking a deep breath, "you are the dearest, sweetest, most wonderful man I have ever known, and I love you beyond description."

He let out a rush of air, only then realizing he hardly had been breathing.

"Come here," he growled, holding out his arms.

"Pardon me?" she asked, eyebrows raised innocently.

"Come here!"

She laughed as she literally flung herself at Jace and was caught tightly by his strong arms. He held her against him, leaving her feet to dangle above the floor. She wrapped her arms around his neck and brought her lips to his.

He groaned as their tongues met and twined together slowly, seductively. He slid her down his body in a sensuous journey that stirred his manhood. When Heather's feet reached the floor she was aware of the wobbly condition of her knees and clung to him for support as the kiss grew urgent.

Jace lifted his head and drew a ragged breath.

His eyes were a smoky blue-gray and radiated his desire. The liquid fire of need surged through him as he gazed at Heather, saw the flush of her cheeks, the moist invitation of her slightly parted lips.

"Jace," Heather said, her voice a near whisper, almost a sob, as she trembled in his arms.

The sound of his name spoken so tremulously snapped the last of Jace's control, and with a moan he swung Heather up into his arms and carried her into the bedroom. When he set her on her feet he cupped her face in his hands and kissed her so softly, so sensuously, that she had to grip his arms as a wave of dizziness swept over her.

"I want you so much, so damn much," he said almost desperately.

"Yes. Yes, Jace, I want you too."

They parted only long enough to shed their clothing, then stretched out on the bed. Jace lifted her over him, settling her on top of his rugged frame, then spanned her waist with his hands and brought her forward, enabling him to find the lush fullness of her breasts. He drew one nipple into his mouth, stroking it with his tongue until it was taut, throbbing from his tantalizing foray. Her other breast received the same loving attention, and Heather began to grind her hips against his in the same rhythmic motion of his tormenting tongue. His arousal was hard, heated, thrusting against her.

"Oh, Jace, please!" she gasped, as his hands skimmed over her back and down her buttocks.

He rolled her over and beneath him, resting on his arms and planting nibbling kisses down her throat and across the tops of her breasts.

"Where were you?" he asked, his voice strained.

"Where were I when?" she mumbled.

"When you weren't here." He flicked his tongue over one then the other rosy bud of her breasts.

"I had places to go, people to see. I—Jace!" she cried, as he rested his hand on her stomach, then slowly moved it lower.

"Where?" he asked.

"Oh, yes, right there," she said dreamily as his fingers continued their exquisite journey.

"You are under my power," he said in a dramatically rumbly voice. "You will tell me everything I wish to know. We have ways of dealing with people like you."

"Could you deal with me a little faster? I'm going out of my mind!"

"Talk! Spill the beans! Confess all! I want to know where—Oh, Lord!" He groaned as she danced her finger down his stomach and beyond.

"What was the question?" she asked, then traced a lazy circle around his lips with her tongue.

"I forget," he said, and kissed her hard.

"I love you," she murmured when he lifted his head. "And I want you so much."

"Heather mine," he said, then entered her, driving within her, filling her. He slid his arm under her hips to bring her closer, and she arched her back to meet him in frenzied need. The whimpering sounds of passion coming from her throat excited him more, sending him over the edge of reason. He felt her body reaching, struggling, searching, then close tightly around him as the spasms of ecstasy rippled through her. He shuddered from the force of his own release as he called her name. Collapsing against her, he lay spent, sated, then pushed himself up to look at her.

"Heather," he said, then said no more. His throat was choked with emotion.

"Oh, Jace," she whispered, tears clinging to her lashes. "It was . . . you are . . . I love you so much."

He kissed her lingeringly, then slowly, reluctantly, moved away, pulling her close to his side. He wove his fingers through her curls, pressing her head to his shoulder. His body was free of the ache of desire, but his mind felt as though it were splintering into a million pieces. An icy fear gripped him at the thought of losing Heather, of not having her with him for the remainder of his days. Nothing, *nothing*, must happen to their love, what they had together. He saw his life as a void, as endless hours of loneliness without her. He was shaken to the core, and his hold on Heather tightened.

"Jace, you're crushing me," she said.

"What? Oh, I'm sorry," he said, kissing her on the forehead.

"Is something wrong?"

"No, nothing's wrong. I wish I could find brand-new words to say to you instead of just, 'I love you,' because they suddenly aren't enough. Do you understand what I mean?"

"Yes, I do. I never intended to love again, but then you came into my life, and I'm so glad you're here, Jace."

"I'll never leave you, Heather," he said. If only he knew that *she'd* never leave *him*. The planes, the flying, were still there, hovering between them. Tomorrow she'd watch him climb into a jet and soar out of view. It would bring her one step closer to accepting his world. It just had to!

"Shopping," Heather said suddenly.

"What?"

"That's where I was. I watered the plants at my parents' house, then I went shopping. That's the answer to your question, no, your scream, 'Where in the hell have you been?' "

"I acted like a real idiot, didn't I?"

"You will notice, colonel, that I am not angry," she said, trailing her fingertip through the curly hair on his chest.

"I've never been in love before, so I'm bound to make mistakes and—Heather!" he gasped, as her tongue followed the path of her finger.

"Hmm?"

"You are driving me—Oh, Heather!"

"You're just so-o-o sexy, Dalton," she said, wiggling against him.

"That's it!" he growled, flipping her onto her back. "You're going to get it!"

"I certainly hope so," she said merrily.

Much, much later Heather enclosed Jace's hand in a plastic bag and they showered together, which, Heather told him, was a peak experience and she'd certainly find showering alone a boring event from now on. Jace assured her he'd volunteer his presence, no questions asked. Dinner was steak and salad and a bottle of wine that Jace produced from his apartment. They watched a detective movie on TV, argued about who the murderer was, and shouted their annoyance when they both were wrong. Heather modeled her new cinnamon-colored dress, which clung in all the right places, and Jace whistled his approval. There were only the two of them—sharing, laughing, kissing, and touching. It was heaven.

Later, after they had made magnificent love again, Jace pulled Heather close to his side and tucked the blankets around her shoulders. Smiling, she snuggled against his warm body in a lethargic state of contentment.

"Heather?"

"Hmm?"

"We need to set the alarm for earlier than you usually do, so we can be at the base by seven-thirty."

"Be at the—Oh, I'd forgotten for a while that tomorrow is . . ."

"Heather, don't. I can feel you getting tense. I wouldn't have brought it up tonight if it wasn't for setting the clock."

"Yes, I'll do it," she said. A knot of fear tightened in her stomach as she set the alarm, and she drew a shuddering breath as she moved back to Jace's side. "Hold me, Jace," she whispered. "Just hold me."

He gathered her into the circle of his arms, fitting her body to his and weaving his fingers through her silky curls. All he had to do, he thought, was open his mouth and tell her he'd decided not to fly after all because of his hand. He was the cause of her distress, and he had the ability to restore her peace of mind. But for how long? Only until the next time she was confronted with his flying. Should he postpone her torment? Delay it for as long as possible? Dammit, what was the best thing to do? She was so fragile, felt so small in his arms. What gave him the right to make her so unhappy?

"Heather, honey, listen to me," he said quietly.

"Yes?"

"About tomorrow. I—" He stopped abruptly. Was he wrong to push her like this? he wondered. Should he leave her alone? Allow her to exist in a type of fantasy world, pretending he wasn't a pilot and was simply crazy about the color blue? No, that was no good. Games caught up with people, prices eventually had to be paid. Heather had to accept the fact that he flew airplanes for a living, whether he stayed in the Air Force or not. But what if her fears destroyed her love? What if he lost her? "I love you," he said. "Please don't forget that I love you."

"I won't, Jace. I love you too."

"It's only a takeoff and landing, Heather."

"I know, Jace," she said softly. "I know. But I can't help remembering that when Russ was killed in that B-52, he was attempting to land."

Jace clenched his jaw and gently stroked her smooth back. Long after she had drifted off to sleep, he lay awake in the dark, quiet room. His Heather, he thought. She filled a part of his being he hadn't known was empty. He desired her as no woman before, and she evoked protective instincts he hadn't been aware he possessed. Her tears ripped at his soul, and her smile brought a warmth that melted the inner chill of loneliness. Loneliness that had been a part of him for so long, he'd accepted it without question. Until now. Until Heather.

He'd known fear before. When a plane he was testing suddenly went out of control he'd felt that cold ache of fright seep through his veins. But the fear of losing Heather went deeper. It touched his soul and left him shaken. No, it couldn't, *wouldn't* happen. He was the Eagle Catcher, and Heather was the most important mission he had ever had. She was his life.

"I love you, Heather," he said to the night. "Oh, how I do love you."

Eight

Jace kissed Heather awake the next morning before the alarm went off. She mumbled something less than coherent, then gasped as his hand slid lazily across her stomach and up to her breast, his thumb flicking the nipple to an exquisite hardness. In a hazy state that was a combination of sleepiness and heightening passion, she welcomed him into her embrace, and then her body. Their thrusting movements carried them high above reality until they crashed onto the glorious shore of ecstasy. Slowly drifting back as heartbeats quieted, they shared one more loving kiss before Jace moved away.

"Did I say good morning?" he asked.

"Nope," she said, then yawned. "Not verbally, but very nicely."

"Good morning, Heather mine."

"Hi," she said, stretching her arms above her head.

"Well, all good things and whatever," he said, swinging his feet to the floor. "Up! I'll go to my place and shower. Meet me over there in twenty minutes and I'll treat you to my world-famous coffee."

" 'Kay."

"Heather, wake up!"

"Don't yell!"

Jace chuckled as he pulled on his clothes, then kissed Heather on the end of the nose and strode from the room. By the time he was standing under the streaming water in his shower he was frowning. He shook his head ruefully as he considered the importance resting on his flying this morning. It was as though he was about to be the first man on the moon, or some other momentous event. The most simple takeoff and landing could have a tremendous impact on his relationship with the woman he loved. If Heather could witness this flight and push aside the fear that kept creeping in around her, they would take vast steps forward.

"Forward to where?" he muttered as he dried off. Oh, yes, he knew where he wanted them to go. He saw it all so clearly in his mind—Heather as his wife, the mother of his baby. He wanted to marry Heather Wade and spend the rest of his life with her. And today could bring him that much closer to that dream. She could see him fly, and when he was safely back on the ground he would pull her into his arms, kiss and hold her. He'd place her hand on his heart, show her he was alive, and that no harm had come to him because of the flight. They could talk about the future because she'd realize they had one.

"Tonight," he said aloud. "Tonight I ask Heather to marry me." She was going to be uptight this morning and he'd be loose, jolly, he decided firmly. Jolly? That was a bit much. He'd be . . . cheerful. Everything was going to be fine. It just had to be.

Heather showered, then surveyed her closet. What did one wear when watching the man one loved risk his life? No, she mustn't think morbid thought. She had to go to that base with a positive attitude. Jace was trying so hard to help her overcome her fears. He was doing it for her, for them, and she had to do her part. So much was resting on her ability to accept Jace's flying, the planes, the life he had chosen. She had to conquer her fear. She had to!

She chose a flared brown wool skirt with a matching jacket and a rust-colored blouse. After applying light makeup, flicking her curls around her face with a brush, and pushing her feet into brown heels, she took a deep, steadying breath and walked to Jace's apartment.

He greeted her with a sensuous kiss that turned her knees to jelly, then led her to the kitchen. He handed her a mug of coffee and motioned her into a chair at the table.

"Want some toast or something?" he asked. "No, forget that. My bread is hard as a rock."

"Why?"

"I dumped it out so I could use the bag to cover my hand in the shower. I now have about fifteen sliced hockey pucks."

She smiled. "Not bright, colonel."

"Oh, well." He shrugged. "We have to hit the road anyway. I'll tell Ed to buy you some breakfast at the officers' club."

"I'm really not hungry, Jace." She finished her coffee. "I'm going to need a pass to get on base, aren't I?"

"No, you'll be with me."

"But I'm driving my own car."

"What? No, you're not."

"Jace, don't be silly. Why should you have to bring me all the way back? I'm sure you have to get right to work on the X-82 after you fly, and I'll go on to the travel agency myself."

He frowned. "I don't think that's a great idea."

"You know it's the most efficient way to do this. I'll see you after you land, assure you that I'm perfectly fine, then we'll meet up again tonight for dinner. I don't need you to hold my hand all the way into town. Honestly, this is a sound plan."

"Are you sure?"

"Absolutely. Jace, I'm nervous, frightened, and I admit that. But I also know I am very determined to come through this like a champ. You do your part and I'll do mine. Okay?"

"Oh, Heather," he said, covering her hand with

his, "I love you so much. This morning is very important to us, to our future."

"I know that, Jace," she said softly.

Their eyes met and held, sending messages of love, warmth, tenderness. They smiled, and time lost all meaning. There was only the two of them cloaked in a rosy cloud of euphoria. Then delicious sensations of desire crept in around them, and heartbeats quickened.

Jace chuckled and shook his head. "Oh, Heather," he said. "What you do to me simply by looking at me with those fawn's eyes of yours is incredible."

"You're rather potent yourself," she said. "I'm having very naughty thoughts."

"Put them on temporary hold. We'd better go. If we get separated in traffic, park at the visitor's building outside the gate and I'll get you a pass. Listen, I really can bring you back to the travel agency."

"No, this is fine. It really is."

They stood, and Jace wrapped his arms around her and held her, simply held her, for a long moment.

This was where she wanted to stay, Heather thought dreamily, thrilling to the heat and strength of his muscular body. Right here, in the strong arms of Jace Dalton. Forever.

In the parking lot Jace opened the door to Heather's car, then bent down to kiss her after she slid behind the wheel. He waited until she had backed out, then followed in the sports car. The early-morning traffic was heavy, but he managed to keep her in his view as they drove across town.

Damn, he thought, now he was getting butter-flies like some rookie pilot. It was just so important that everything went perfectly. Well, no problem. He could fly a T-38 in his sleep. It was a slick, finely tuned machine that responded to his touch like a willing woman. Everything would be fine.

So far, so good, Heather thought as she stopped at a red light. Her stomach hurt, and Jace's lousy coffee hadn't helped any, but she was hanging in there. Jace was a good pilot, the best. She'd stay calm, cool, and collected. Everything would be fine.

In the small building outside the gate, Jace signed the necessary papers to obtain a pass for Heather. Then he instructed her to follow him, saying they were headed for the Operations Building.

"*Ops,*" she said. "I know all about your fancy jargon, colonel."

Jace laughed as they got back into their cars. Ed Turner was waiting for them when they arrived at the Operations Building. He saluted Jace, then kissed Heather's hand after Jace had introduced them.

" 'Mornin', my sweet magnolia pie," Ed drawled. "You have brought such beauty to this vast waste-land that it brings tears to this Southern boy's eyes."

"Put a cork in it, major," Jace said, laughing.

"Well, darn," Heather said. "He was just getting warmed up. Why don't you ever say marvelous things like that to me, Jace?"

"Oh, hell," Jace growled as Ed dissolved in a fit of laughter.

Inside the building Jace encircled Heather's shoulders with his arm and smiled down at her.

"Okay?" he asked.

"Okay," she said, returning his smile.

"Go on upstairs to the tower, Ed. After I take off, buy Heather some breakfast."

"Yes, suh, colonel, suh. My pleasure."

"Ed, I want you to take care of—"

"Jace," Ed interrupted, "don't worry about a thing."

"Yeah, well, I—"

"Jace, I'm fine," Heather said, placing her hand on his arm.

"I love you, Heather," he said, brushing his lips over hers. "See you soon."

"Roger," she said, smiling.

Heather watched as Jace strode away and disappeared through a door on the opposite side of the room. Her smile faded and she slid her tongue nervously over her bottom lip.

She didn't want to be here, she thought frantically. Ghosts would be dredged up to haunt her. Ghosts of loneliness, of fear. She would remember when they came to tell her that Russ was dead. Ready, ready now? No, she wasn't. She wasn't ready to open old wounds and relive the past. She only wanted Jace. But that wasn't going to happen if she didn't accept the uniform and the planes along with the man. She had to calm down. Now!

"Let's go upstairs, sweet lady," Ed said.

"What? Oh, yes, of course."

The glass-enclosed tower gave a spectacular view of the mountains and desert, but Heather's gaze was riveted on the needle-nosed T-38 jet fighter sitting on the ramp below. The sun shimmered over the silver aircraft, giving it an almost eerie, iridescent glow. The knot in her stomach tightened and she pressed her fingertips to her temples.

"Easy does it, magnolia pie," Ed said.

"Jace says he's a good pilot."

"The best, darlin'. The best in this man's Air Force. Watching him fly is a thing of beauty. They've been after him for years to join the Thunderbirds, the precision flying team, but he's not interested in being the entertainment. Jace feels he has a job to do, something to accomplish."

"He'd never be happy if he gave up flying, would he?" she asked quietly.

"No, he wouldn't. He'll hang up his wings when he's too old to soar, but not before. He wouldn't be Jace if he wasn't flying."

"I'm glad you're with me," she said, managing a weak smile. "Thank you, Ed."

"You bet, darlin'."

"Jace is a good pilot. Yes, he's the best there is," she said, staring down at the plane again.

Ed frowned as he looked at Heather's pale face, but kept silent.

"How's that, colonel?" an airman asked.

"That ought to do it," Jace said, flexing his fingers. "Thanks for the first aid."

"I hope you don't pop those stitches, sir."

"The gauze pad and tape should protect them. I'm not doing anything fancy up there today. Just disturbing the birds."

Jace stood and tugged up the zipper on the olive-green flight suit he wore. A black leather square over his left pocket stated his name and rank in silver letters, and he wore black boots on his feet. He tucked a helmet with a dark green visor under his arm and left the building.

"Pretty, pretty plane," he said under his breath as he approached the T-38.

He saluted in the direction of the tower, picturing Heather in his mind, then nodded to the crew chief, who placed a ladder against the side of the plane. Jace climbed up, then eased himself into the cockpit. The crew chief leaned forward and strapped him in. Jace put on his helmet, then slipped the visor into place.

"Have a good flight, colonel," the crew chief said. "Make this baby sing."

Jace gave him a thumb's up sign, then pressed the button to lower the canopy. As he aligned the thin wire of the microphone, he turned it on.

"Williams tower," he said, "this is Eagle Catcher. Ready for takeoff. Over."

"Jace," Heather said, spinning around as his voice came over the transmitter on the other side of the room. "That's Jace."

"Yes, it's him," Ed said. "The Eagle Catcher."

"Roger, Eagle Catcher," the traffic controller said. "You're cleared to taxi to the end of the runway."

"Roger," Jace said.

Heather wrapped her arms about her waist and chewed on the inside of her cheek as the two turbojets on the T-38 roared to life with a high-pitched whine. Jace nudged the plane forward onto the taxi strip, then came to a complete stop.

"You're okay to go, Eagle Catcher," the controller said.

"Roger."

As the plane started down the runway the afterburners burst with fire, thrusting the aircraft forward like a panther at last released from its restraining leash. After going only a few thousand feet the plane lifted off the ground in a smooth, powerful motion.

"Oh no, Jace. Don't!" Heather whispered.

"Heather," Ed said gently, "he's up. It was a perfect takeoff. Picture perfect. Look at him soar, Heather. It's beautiful."

Heather nodded slightly, watching as the plane became a tiny speck in the sky, then disappeared from view. She slowly let out a trembling breath and turned to face Ed Turner.

"I believe you were going to buy me some breakfast, major," she said, her voice unsteady as she lifted her chin to a determined tilt.

Ed grinned. "You bet I am, darlin' girl. The finest in the place. Let's go."

In the crowded cafeteria, Heather and Ed placed

their trays on a table by the window and ate in silence for several minutes. Heather was amazed to discover that she actually was hungry, and that the tight knot of fear in her stomach had vanished. All she had to do now was watch Jace land and she would have come through the ordeal just fine. It was half over.

"Ed," she said, replacing her coffee cup in the saucer, "is there a special significance behind Jace's code name?"

"The Eagle Catcher? Oh, yes, ma'am, there sure is. See, when Jace was a rookie pilot, it didn't take long for everyone to figure out he had the golden arm. He was tagged the Eagle, because he soared like one. I didn't know him then, but I'd heard plenty of stories about the Eagle. I knew I was in good company when I was assigned to his fighter squadron in 'Nam. Jace's crew chief was a full-blooded Shoshone Indian named Ten."

"Ten?"

"It was short for something nobody could pronounce. We just called him Ten. He was quiet, I mean, quiet! That guy said one word a week if he was feeling real chatty. One night we came back late from a mission, tired but geared up, wired, so we went to the mess tent to have some coffee and unwind. There was a bunch of us sitting there, and all of a sudden ol' Ten opens his mouth and starts talkin'. Nearly scared us out of our shorts."

"What did he say?"

"He said that Jace was the Eagle Catcher. He said that in the early days of the Shoshone, a brave

warrior would hide among the rocks on a mountain and catch a live eagle in his bare hands. If he
lived through it, he was wealthy in valuable eagle
feathers, and rich in tribal honors. He was the
finest of his kind, the best. Ten said Jace was like
the Eagle Catcher because he was in command of
everything when he piloted a plane. Jace was the
best, and deserved to have the title."

"That's an incredible story," Heather said,
brushing a sudden tear from her cheek.

"No joke. We all were choked up that night, let
me tell you. Then, before Jace could say anything,
Ten got up and walked out. I swear, he didn't speak
again for six months. He'd used himself up on that
one shot. But from then on Jace was the Eagle
Catcher. Helluva name for a helluva guy. 'Course,
the title is yours now."

"I beg your pardon?"

"You've caught the Eagle, darlin'. *You* are the
Eagle Catcher. You've got Jace sewed up but good,
the lucky devil."

"Well, I'm not sure I'm the Eagle Catcher," she
said, smiling, "but thank you for telling me the
story."

"You bet. Let's finish up and get back to the
tower. Jace will be landing soon. You're doin'
A-OK, magnolia pie."

When Heather and Ed returned to the tower Ed
introduced her to another officer there, Major Jim
Clemens.

"So, what's got you up here, Jim?" Ed asked.

"A baby chick on his first solo in a T-38," Jim

said. "I feel like a nervous father every time I go through this."

"How's he doin'?"

"Great. He's my top student. Flies like a pro, an ace. He'll be landing pretty quick here."

"Williams tower, this is Eagle Catcher," came the voice from the transmitter. "Requesting permission to approach for landing. Over."

"Hold up, Eagle Catcher. We're bringing Baby Chick in ahead of you. Over."

"Roger. I see him below me. Over."

"Williams tower, this is Baby Chick. Requesting permission to—Oh, my God!" The pilot's voice rose on a note of panic. "I've lost an engine!"

Heather's eyes widened and she stared in horror at Ed.

"Baby Chick, this is Williams Tower," the controller said, his voice steady. "What is—"

"I'm going to eject!" the pilot interrupted frantically.

"No!" Jace's voice, calm and soothing, broke in. "You're too low, Baby Chick. Do not, I repeat, do not eject!"

"Dear God," Heather whispered.

"Easy, darlin'," Ed said.

Jim strode to the transmitter. "Baby Chick, this is Major Clemens. That plane above you is piloted by Colonel Dalton. Listen to him, Willie. Do everything he says. Colonel, he's all yours. Over."

"Roger," Jace said. "Willie, this is Colonel Dalton."

"The Eagle Catcher?" Willie said, his voice trembling slightly.

"Roger," Jace said. "Just take it easy. We're going to pretend we're the Thunderbirds, Willie. I'm coming down to your right wing."

"I've only got one engine, sir! I'll hit the reset button and—"

"No! You ate a bird when you flew through that big flock back there. Don't hit the reset or you'll have a fire."

"No," Heather said, tears misting her eyes. "No."

"It's okay," Ed said, encircling her shoulders with his arm. "Jace has everything under control."

"Hit the right rudder, Willie," they heard Jace say. "Level out your wings. That's it. A little more. I'm right beside you."

"Get the fire trucks on the runway," Jim said to one of the men there, who immediately snatched up a phone.

Heather was aware of the metallic taste of fear in her mouth as she watched the trucks streak to the runway and line up along its edge. Her eyes scanned the heavens in a frantic search for the two planes.

Jace! her mind screamed as her heart battered wildly against her ribs. It all was to have been so simple, and now. . .

"There they are!" Ed yelled as the planes came into view. "Jace is hugging his wing like a mother hen. That is sweet flying!"

"If Willie veers off, they'll both go down," Jim said. "Damn that kid! He's the last one I'd figure would panic. I've never had an ace crumble on me before."

"Oh, Jace!" Heather whispered, pressing her fingers to her lips. "Don't! Don't!"

"Okay, Willie," Jace said, his voice low and even, "shut that engine down completely."

"But—"

"Do it, son."

"Yes, sir. Yes, sir, I did."

"Lower the landing gear manually. Grab the handle, Willie."

Heather watched in terror as the two jets roared past the tower. Jace was so close to the other aircraft, they almost appeared to be one. His image danced before her eyes, tormenting her—his smile, his dark, silky hair, the clear blue of his eyes. Her Jace. Her beloved Jace. And now he was going to die.

A moan escaped from her throat as tears rolled down her cheeks. Ed was speaking to her in a low, soothing voice, but she heard only a rush of noise in her ears as she was held tightly in an internal battle with icy fear.

Jace was going to die, she thought hazily, and she was helpless. She couldn't beat the planes. They had killed Russ, and now they were going to take Jace from her. She had pretended it wouldn't happen because she loved him so much, wanted to be with him forever. But it was over. Any minute now, any second, her beloved Jace would be dead.

"Let's turn these babies around," Jace's voice came over the transmitter. "Easy, Willie. That's it.

We'll go to the end of the strip for a landing approach. Straighten your wings. Good. Williams tower, requesting clearance for Baby Chick to land. Over."

"Roger," the controller said. "Bring it on home."

As the two planes circled in tight synchronization, a strained silence fell over the people in the tower. Below, on the ground, groups of men stood still as statues, gazes turned to the sky. It was as though time had stopped.

"Okay, Willie," Jace said, "take it in slow and easy. I'll be right beside you. Thanks for the ride, son. You did a helluva fine job."

"Yes, sir. Thank you, sir. I'm approaching the runway."

As Willie's plane touched down on the runway, Jace veered off in a tight bank to the right, then shot upward, engines shrieking as he gained altitude.

"All right!" Jim yelled as Willie's plane slowed to a stop. "He's down!"

"Amen," Ed said, letting out a long breath.

Jim ran from the tower to meet his young pilot as the other men smiled and slapped each other on the back. The crisis was over.

Heather was numb. She seemed to have floated away from herself, watching the drama unfold in foggy, detached fascination. Unnoticed tears continued to stream down her face as she stared out the window.

"Williams tower, this is Eagle Catcher," she

heard Jace say. "Requesting permission to land. Over."

"You've got it. We'd bring in a brass band if we had one handy. Over."

"Roger," Jace said, and chuckled.

"He's laughing?" Heather said, snapping out of her trance and spinning around to face Ed. "He nearly died, and he thinks it's funny?"

"Heather, calm down."

"Where is the humor in this?" she asked, her voice rising. "Is it a joke because he cheated death this time? Score one for Jace? It's all a crazy game to him, isn't it? Roulette with death. That's his world, those planes, the thrill of winning another round. That's what he really loves!"

"Heather, don't!" Ed said. "Let's go downstairs. You'll see for yourself that Jace is fine. See, he's on the ground. It's over."

"Yes, Ed," she said, a chilling calmness sweeping through her. "It's over."

Jace shut down the engines, popped the canopy, and unhooked his harness. As he tugged off his helmet, he let out a long, weary sigh. Sweat trickled down his face, back, and chest, and his hair was plastered to his head. The adrenaline that had surged through his body was gone now, and he felt enervated. The crew chief set the ladder in place, and Jace pushed himself slowly upward, every muscle aching with fatigue.

Dear Lord, he thought as he climbed down, one

wrong move by that kid and they both would have crashed. And Heather had seen it all. He had done what he had to do, but . . . Dammit to hell! Why today? Why had it happened today? He had to get to her, see how she was, show her he was alive and everything was fine.

"Helluva flight, sir," the crew chief said, snapping Jace from his anguished thoughts.

"Yeah, a barrel of laughs," he said, frowning.

"You saved the kid's neck. He was damn lucky it was you up there with him. Major Clemens took him into Ops. I guess you'll have tons of paperwork to fill out on this one. It was really something."

"Yeah," Jace said. "It sure was."

He looked up toward the tower, then over to the group of men who were watching him as he walked forward. There was no sign of either Heather or Ed, and a knot tightened in his stomach.

"Base newspaper, sir," a man said, rushing up to him. "Do you have any comment to make on what happened up there, colonel?"

"No," Jace said. "No comment."

"But, colonel, you saved—"

"No comment!" he growled, pushing past the reporter and yanking open the door to the Operations Building.

The buzzing of voices stopped as Jace entered, and all heads turned in his direction. A young man clad in a flight suit made his way forward, saluting as he stopped in front of Jace.

"Colonel, sir, I—I'm Willie McBride. I just wanted

to thank you, sir, for saving my life up there and I—" He stopped, emotion choking off his words.

"You did all right, Willie," Jace said, placing his hand on the younger man's shoulder. "As for me, I was scared to death."

"You? Oh, no, sir, not the Eagle Catcher."

Jace smiled. "Believe it. I feel about a hundred years old. We gave them a pretty good show, though, I guess. Don't ever be ashamed to admit fear, Willie. Understand?"

"Yes, sir. Thank you, sir."

Jace returned Willie's salute, then continued across the room, his eyes roaming over the throng for Heather and Ed. He nodded absently in response to the congratulations, then realized someone had shoved into his hand a stack of papers that needed to be filled out regarding the incident.

Where was she? Jace wondered, feeling a rush of panic. Where was Heather?

"Jace!" Ed called, running across the room.

"Dammit, Ed, where is she?" Jace roared.

"I tried to stop her," Ed said, gasping for breath, "but she wouldn't listen to me. Damm it, Jace, I didn't know what to do!"

"Where is she?"

"She left. She got in her car and drove away. Jace, I'm sorry."

Jace drew a shuddering breath and stared at the ceiling for a long moment, a haunted pain settling in the depths of his eyes.

"I've got to go after her," he said, his voice raspy. "I've to to talk to her, tell her . . ."

"No, Jace," Ed said. "She needs some room, some space. I don't think there's anything you could say right now that would help. Leave her alone for a while."

"I'm going to lose her, Ed," he said softly. "I'm going to lose my Heather."

Nine

Heather hardly remembered driving away from the base. Ed had pleaded with her to stay, to see Jace, but she had refused, unable to speak as tears choked her. She drove, not caring where she was going, knowing only that she had to get away, far away, from the planes.

The battle had been fought and she had lost. Icy misery swept through her as she admitted her defeat. Over and over she replayed in her mind the scene she had witnessed in the tower—Jace in the silver jet as he hugged the wing of the frightened young pilot, Jace risking his life, then his chuckle when he'd cheated death one more time.

That was Jace's world, she thought, brushing tears from her cheeks. The planes, the excitement, the challenge of the heavens, of the aircraft versus anything that would send it plummeting to the ground. He was the Eagle Catcher, the best of his kind. He lived to fly, not to love.

"I can't do it," she whispered. "I can't!"

As tears blurred her vision she drove aimlessly through winding streets until she saw a small park. A few minutes later she sank onto a bench beneath a tree and dropped her face into her trembling hands. The tears flowed endlessly as she cried for Jace, for the man she loved so deeply. She cried for what they might have had. And she cried because she was beaten, had struggled to win against the fear and had lost. She felt empty, drained, and incredibly alone.

With hands clutched tightly in her lap, feeling masochistic and not caring, she relived every precious moment she had shared with Jace Dalton. Their lovemaking was a vivid memory, and she welcomed the flush of desire that heated her, savoring it one last time. She had come alive under Jace's tender kiss and touch, had truly become a woman capable of the giving of herself to her man. Jace had awakened her femininity as never before.

She saw his smile, heard his laughter. Every steely muscle of his magnificent body was etched indelibly in her mind. And then she tucked each memory away in a special section of her heart and soul, and said good-bye. Good-bye to Jace, whom she would love for the remainder of her days.

Heather stayed in the quiet park, not having the energy to move. With an aching heart, she sat alone and thought of Jace.

*　　*　　*

The remainder of the morning was a series of frustrating hours for Jace. His mind was centered on Heather and his need for her. He could imagine the fear she had experienced because of the incident with the rookie pilot. He wanted to assure her that everything was fine, that he was well, that no harm had come to him. It had been tense as he'd guided Willie in, but he had known what he was doing, had taken no unnecessary risks.

Heather had run from him, from the planes, from his world, and he needed to find her, tell her he loved her, that he wanted to marry her so they could be together always. Where had she gone? What was she thinking? The questions beat against his brain as he filled out the report, and he had to reread the forms time and again as his mind wandered to Heather.

At last he strode into the locker room and stripped off his sweat-soaked flight suit for a much-needed shower. When he pulled the tape and the gauze pad from his hand he swore in disgust as he saw the oozing blood and the stitches that had been ripped out. After showering and dressing in his uniform he asked Ed to drive him to the infirmary, where the stitches were repaired and Jace's hand rewrapped in a heavy layer of gauze.

"Let's go to the office," Jace said to Ed, getting back into the car.

"We're due at the hangar, Jace."

"The office, Ed!" he barked. "I've got to find out if Heather got to the travel agency all right."

"Yeah, okay." Ed frowned. "Helluva morning, huh?"

"The greatest of my life," Jace muttered. "I could wring that Willie's neck! Oh, hell, it wasn't his fault. It wasn't anyone's fault. But the fact remains that it happened, it blew Heather away, and I don't even know where she is. I've got to see her, Ed, before she makes up her mind to end it between us."

"You're on duty all day."

"I don't give a damn!"

"Oh, boy," Ed moaned. "You're acting crazy, Jace."

Jace muttered a few well-chosen expletives, and Ed drove to the office without another word. Bruce was nowhere to be found, and Ed speculated aloud that the aide was no doubt waiting in the hangar with the rest of the X-82 crew. Jace ignored Ed, looked up the number of Wishing Well Travel, and dialed it on the telephone.

"Wishing Well Travel," a woman said.

"Heather Wade, please."

"I'm sorry, she isn't in. May I take a message?"

"Lori?"

"Yes."

"This is Jace Dalton. I realize you don't know me, but—"

"I feel as though I do, Jace," she interrupted. "Where's Heather? I know she was going out to the base with you this morning, but I expected her back by now. Is anything wrong?"

"There was a problem during my flight, Lori. Heather became very upset and left before I could see her. I don't know where she went."

"Oh, no."

"I'm out of my mind with worry. Can you think of anyplace Heather might have gone?"

"No, not really. Have you tried her apartment?"

"Not yet, but I will. I've got to find her!"

"Take it easy, Jace. Heather has just gone somewhere to think things through."

"Look, I'll call you later to see if you've heard from her, okay?"

"Yes, of course."

"I'll check in with you soon."

"All right. 'Bye, Jace."

A call to Heather's apartment afforded nothing but the sound of the telephone ringing over and over in Jace's ear, and he finally slammed the receiver back into place.

"Jace," Ed said, coming into the office, "you'd better take a look at this."

"What is it?" he asked absently, as he drummed his fingers on the desk.

"The report from Langley on Russ Wade's crash in the B-52."

"And?" Jace said, straightening in his chair.

"Read it," Ed said. "It answers a lot of questions about what's going on with Heather and the planes. A helluva lot!"

"Let me see that."

"I'll go down to the hangar and get started. Come when you're ready. You can't do anything on the simulator with that hand, anyway."

"What? Oh. Yeah, okay," Jace mumbled, his gaze riveted to the papers in front of him.

A short time later Jace let out a long breath and sank back in his chair. His mind was whirling from the impact of what he had read in the report on Russ Wade, but one thought came through the maze loud and clear. He had to find Heather.

He called her apartment again, but got no answer, nor had Lori heard from Heather. Twenty minutes later Jace strode into the hangar and shoved a piece of paper at Ed.

"What's this?" Ed asked.

"A release from the doctor saying I'm in no shape to work the simulator because of my hand. If the general hollers, show him that. I'm going after Heather."

"Lord, Jace, I've never seen you like this."

"I'm fighting for my life, Ed," Jace said, turning away. "That's what she is to me. My life, my reason for being."

"Then go get her, Eagle Catcher," Ed called after him. "And good luck."

Jace's entire body was tensed as he drove into the parking lot at the apartment building. A muscle twitched in his jaw when he saw that Heather's car was not in its designated slot. Upstairs in his living room he called Lori, was told she had not heard from Heather, then gave Lori his home telephone number. After changing into jeans and a black sweater he left his door ajar and waited for Heather to return.

Two hours later Heather stepped out of the elevator and walked down the hall toward her apartment. She knew Jace was home because she had seen his car in the lot, and had almost driven away again rather than see him. But, she had decided, there was no point in postponing the inevitable, in delaying saying aloud the farewell that had been tearing at her soul the entire day. It was over, all of it, and nothing could change that now.

Jace stepped into the hall just as she passed his door and she stopped, looking up at him with a sad, weary expression on her face.

"Hello, Jace," she said quietly.

"We have to talk, Heather."

"Yes," she said, continuing on to her own apartment. She unlocked the door and stepped inside with Jace right behind her. "There really isn't a lot to say," she said, turning to face him. "I tried to accept your world, your planes, but I wasn't strong enough. I lost the battle, Jace. It's over. I love you. I will always love you, but we have no future together. I've cried until there are no more tears. I just want you to go and leave me alone. It won't work for us. You know it and I know it."

"No, I *don't* know it," he said, crossing his arms over his broad chest. "What I *do* know is that our future together, or lack of it, is being determined by a ghost, by a man who was killed three years ago. Russ Wade is the enemy here, Heather, not the planes. Everything could have gone like clockwork at the base, and you still would have run from me."

"You're not making any sense," she said, sinking down onto the sofa.

"Aren't I?" he said, coming to stand in front of her. "I could never figure out why you kept harping on whether or not I was a good pilot. You kept bringing it up, over and over. I told you I was good, but you'd still dwell on it. Why, Heather? Why did you keep having to reassure yourself that I had the ability and the common sense to fly those planes in such a way that I could get back on the ground in one piece?"

"Because I love you, and I just needed to know that you—"

"No!" he said, his voice rising. "You've buried it all so deeply inside of you that you're not facing the truth. But it would sneak in on you, show itself in the form of that question you kept asking me."

"I don't know what you're talking about!"

"Yes, you do! It's not the planes you're afraid of, Heather, it's the man piloting them!"

"No. No!"

"Listen to me," he said, gripping her by the upper arms and hauling her to her feet. "You panicked today because it all came rushing back. You were seeing a situation that was out of the ordinary, not going as it was supposed to. It tumbled together in your mind, didn't it? You weren't sure if I was flying like a pro, or like some hot shot, putting mine and that kid's life in danger with my theatrics. Isn't that right, Heather? Isn't it?"

"No! No! Yes! Oh, God, I don't know," she sobbed, tears spilling onto her cheeks.

"Yes, you do! Russ was a hotdog pilot. He was written up twice for hassling, playing dangerous dogfight war games with other pilots, which is totally against regulations. The night he was flying that B-52 he disregarded his orders to divert to another airfield because of the storm. He decided to show them how great he was. He crashed that Buff and killed himself and everyone on board."

"No!" she screamed.

"Yes! Oh, Heather, don't you see? It's not the uniform or the planes that are haunting you. You're blaming them rather than facing the truth about the man you married. He was shallow and selfish and cared only about himself. His attitude cost him his life, and it took the lives of others. He was the one you had chosen to love, and he wasn't what you believed him to be. You buried it, Heather, ran from the past, then shifted it around in your mind until you could deal with it."

"No! Don't say anymore! You don't know what you're talking about."

"All of it's true," he said quietly, dropping his hands and stepping back. "It's Russ that's keeping us apart, not my flying. The man is dead, and you're living his guilt for him. There's no more I can do, Heather. I love you. Lord, how I love you." His voice was choked with emotion. "But until you look deep within yourself and face the truth we don't have any chance of a life together."

"You're wrong!" she shrieked. "I hate those planes, that uniform, I hate—"

"All right," he interrupted, and weariness and defeat filled his eyes. "I won't force you to hear it again. I'm moving out to the base so I won't be around to remind you of the hurt I've caused you. I was fighting for us, Heather, for our love, our future. We couldn't go on like this, with Russ's ghost between us, but I guess I've lost you anyway by being the one who made you face the truth."

"It isn't the truth!"

"Good-bye, Heather," he said softly, walking to the door. "I'll always love you. Always. I'm sorry I made you cry. I'll never forgive myself for that. Beautiful fawn's eyes shouldn't be sad."

He turned to look at her one last time, and their eyes met and held for a long moment. Then, with a shuddering breath that seemed to rip at his very soul, he left the apartment, shutting the door quietly behind him.

"No," Heather whispered, reaching out to grab the sofa as her legs gave way beneath her. "Russ didn't kill himself and those other men. It was the plane, the damnable plane! Planes are the killers! Jace is wrong! Wrong!"

She sank to her knees and buried her face in her hands as the sobs racked her body. The image of Jace danced before her eyes, then Russ's face, then planes, and rows and rows of men in blue uniforms. With a strangled moan, she stumbled to her feet and went into her bedroom, flinging herself across the bed and crying until at last, in total exhaustion, she slept, huddled in a ball like a frightened child.

Jace braced his hands on the windowframe in his office and stared out at the star-studded sky. His mind skittered to where he knew it would go, and he saw her face before him. Heather.

One month. It had been one aching, lonely month since he'd walked out of her apartment, and the pain within him at the loss of the only woman he had ever loved had grown greater with every passing day.

"Jace?" Ed said from the doorway.

"Yeah?"

"Ready to knock off?"

"No, not yet."

"Come on, man, you can't keep pushing yourself like this." Ed crossed the room to him. "You skipped dinner again and you look like hell. Jace, you've got to snap out of it. I know you miss Heather, but—"

"Miss her?" Jace said, turning to face him. "I love her. I love her so damn much, and I was the one who twisted the knife in her."

"You told her the truth! Russ Wade was a hotdog! If he hadn't been killed that night, they'd have taken his wings away from him. He didn't deserve to fly. Heather was given the facts at the time of his death, and she chose not to face them. You did the right thing, Jace. You couldn't live with her with Wade's ghost hovering around."

"Heather has it all tangled up with the planes, Ed," Jace said, his voice rising. "If I remove the planes, I get rid of Russ Wade."

"What are you saying?"

"Nothing, *nothing*, means anything without her. Three days from now I fly the X-82 for the whole country to see, and I don't give a damn! Heather is my life! I'm not reenlisting, Ed. I'm leaving the service when these last few months are up, and I'll never fly a plane again. I'm going to go to Heather and promise her that I'll never fly again, then beg her to come back to me."

"Not fly? You? Jace, you'll never be happy if you give it up. Never."

"I need my Heather, Ed," he said quietly. "If it means giving up flying to have her, then I'll do it. I swear I will."

"That won't be necessary, Jace," a soft voice said.

Jace and Ed spun around to face the figure standing in the doorway.

"Heather?" Jace said. "Heather?"

"Yes, it's me. I—I was on my way to the officers' quarters to find you, then I saw your car, and I . . . Jace, I . . ."

"I hear my Southern mama callin' me," Ed said, hurrying to the door. "You're a beautiful sight to see, magnolia pie," he added, kissing Heather on the cheek as he made a hasty exit.

"Heather," Jace said, starting toward her.

"No, please." She raised her hand to silence him as she moved into the room. "There's so much I have to say to you, so much to beg your forgiveness for."

"Heather, no! You—"

"Jace, I went to Langley."

"What?"

"I went there, and I watched the B-52s fly. I saw the pilots, the planes, the house where Russ and I lived. I stood on the sidewalk in front of that little house, and I remembered the officers coming to tell me that Russ was dead."

"Oh, Heather, why did you put yourself through that? Why?"

"I had to know, Jace. I had to know the truth. They came back, you see, the officers, a week later, when I was supposedly over my shock. That's the part I had erased from my mind, refused to hear or believe. They told me about Russ disobeying orders that night and that the crash was caused by pilot error, was Russ's fault. I never told anyone, not even my parents or Lori. I returned here and started my life over. I couldn't accept the truth about Russ, so I blamed the planes, the Air Force. I was lying to myself all those years, Jace."

"I shouldn't have done it," he said, his voice breaking. "I didn't have the right to cause you such pain. I'm so sorry!"

"You were fighting for us, for our love, just as you said. You freed me from . . . from myself. Oh, Jace, I love you so much. I'm sorry I hurt you. I forced you to choose between me and the planes, and that was wrong of me." Tears began streaming down her face. "Oh, Jace, forgive me, please! I need you so. Please, Jace."

With a deep moan, Jace closed the distance between them and pulled her roughly into his arms, burying his face in the fragrant cloud of her hair. She wrapped her arms around his waist, feeling his strength, drinking in his special aroma. He slowly lifted his head and gazed down at her. Tears were glistening in his eyes.

"Promise me you won't quit flying, Jace," Heather said. "You're the Eagle Catcher. You belong in the clouds."

"I'll fly, Heather, but *you*'re the Eagle Catcher. I will love you forever and beyond. Will you marry me, Heather Wade?"

"With loving pride, Jace Dalton," she said, smiling through her tears.

He lowered his head and flicked his tongue along her lips, seeking and gaining entry to the sweet darkness within. With a quiet sob, Heather leaned against him as the kiss intensified and her desire soared. They clung to each other as if they would never again let go. The hurt and loneliness, the confusion and pain, were pushed into oblivion and replaced by loving thoughts and heightening passions.

"I want you, Heather," Jace murmured. "I still have the apartment next to yours. I haven't been there in a month, but . . ."

"Let's go home, colonel," she said. "I am definitely ready, ready now."

"Oh, Heather." Jace sighed. "I do love you."

"And I love you."

Outside the stars twinkled a million hellos overhead as Jace and Heather walked to her car. He opened the door for her, kissed her deeply, then promised to be right behind her in his car during the drive to the apartment.

Heather declared Jace's apartment to be much too musty from being closed up, so they went to hers. Their lovemaking was a celebration of ecstasy, a declaration of their love and lifelong commitment. It was man and woman, Jace and Heather, as one. Through the entire night they reached again and again for each other, kissing, touching, arousing, then joining in the dance of lovers. When they slept they lay close, heads resting on the same pillow, hands entwined.

The next morning Heather opened her eyes to gaze at Jace's face. Oh, how she'd missed him during the past month, she thought. Day and night she had thought of him, aching to be with him. But the seed of doubt that he had placed in her mind on that last fateful night had taken root and slowly grown, and at last she had known she must seek the truth.

She had traveled to Langley Air Force Base, filled with fear at what she might find. She had returned to Phoenix freed from the shackles of that fear. Free to live. And free to love her Jace.

His dark lashes fluttered, then lifted to reveal his crystal-blue eyes.

"Thank heavens," he said huskily. "I was afraid I

might have dreamed all of this, but you're really here."

"To stay, colonel. By the way, what does one do with an eagle once one has caught him? As an official Eagle Catcher, I really ought to know."

"Just love him, sweet magnolia pie," he said, grinning. "Just love him."

"Yes, sir, colonel, sir. I understand perfectly!"

And she carried out her orders.

On the day of the test flight for the X-82 Heather dressed in a cranberry-colored wool skirt and matching sweater, told the butterflies in her stomach to at least fly in synchronization, and drove to the base. Jace had left at dawn for the preflight briefing and last minute procedure check. She had a special pass so that she could sit with Ed and the other members of the crew in specially constructed bleachers. The public was out in force, along with high-ranking military officers, newspaper reporters, and television cameramen.

A murmur went up from the crowd when Jace appeared, flanked by the members of his crew. He stopped by the gleaming jet, saluted the crew, then shook hands with each member in turn. His gaze flickered over the crowd, and a smile tugged at his lips when he saw Heather. She nodded and smiled in return.

Lord, how he loved her, Jace thought. In a few hours they would be married and would begin, really begin, their life together. He would have given up flying for her, but he hadn't had to because she'd beaten the foe and come home to him. Heather. His love.

"You gonna fly this bird, suh?" Ed drawled.

"Yep," Jace said. "Go take care of my lady, corn pone. Tell her I'll be back in a jiffy."

"Yes, suh!"

"Bruce," Jace said, "put the ladder up."

"Me?" Bruce croaked.

Ed chuckled. "It's 'Me, sir.' "

"You, Bruce," Jace said. "It's an important job for a big man."

"Yes, sir!" Bruce said, saluting sharply.

History was made that day on the Arizona desert. Colonel Jace Dalton of the United States Air Force flew the X-82 high above the sun-baked ground and cheering crowd. He maneuvered the silver jet with a golden arm, a sixth sense, the right stuff, the special touch of the Eagle Catcher. He flew it for his country, for himself, and for his lady, who watched with tears of pride and love shimmering in her eyes.

"He flies as sweet as magnolia pie," Heather said, and Ed whooped with delight.

That night, in a bridal suite in Las Vegas, Colonel and Mrs. Jace Dalton lifted their glasses of champagne in a toast to each other.

"I love you, Heather," Jace said, his eyes filled with desire and endless love.

"And I love you, Jace," she whispered.

"Do you suppose we might have a little Eagle Catcher someday soon?"

"Ready, ready now, colonel," she said, smiling warmly.

They soared to a place the X-82 could never go—a private place, a special place known only to them. It was a place above time and space and reality. They lingered there, then drifted back, secure in their love. Later they slept, entwined in each other's arms, dreaming the dreams of lovers.

Both were Eagle Catchers.

Forever.

THE EDITOR'S CORNER

Ah, the crazy calendar of publishing! Here I am recovering from a far too generous Thanksgiving dinner ... having just sent off the December 1986 LOVESWEPTs to be set into galleys ... and preparing to tell you all about our romances for the merry month of May, although they really go on sale the first week of April. Is it any wonder that editors misdate their checks? So, as you can tell, the questionnaires we ran in our books last fall are still reaching us in large numbers as I write this. Here, then, is a quick up-date on your progress report to us about the quality of our stories. 55% of you said the quality has improved; 32% said it has remained the same; only 13% believe the quality has declined. Not bad, huh? Again, thank you so much for going through all the trouble of responding and, of course, for giving us so favorable a progress report. We'll be riding high on your faith in us, and working as hard as ever as we head into our fourth year of publishing LOVESWEPT.

Now, moving right along to those books for the merry month of May (which is really April but went to the printer last ... oh, never mind!). Leading off our exciting quartet of love stories next month is talented Kathleen Creighton with **DELILAH'S WEAKNESS**, LOVESWEPT #139, and what a rip-roarin' good read this is! Heroine Delilah Beaumont is a spunky beauty who is trying to keep a sheep ranch going single-handedly when gorgeous Luke MacGregor crashes into her life ... literally. Surviving her first aid, Luke decides he really wants a *slow* recuperation because Delilah's courage and loveliness have captivated him from his first sight of her. Soon, Ms. Beaumont isn't the least bit eager for him to leave either ... but a completely unexpected link between his interests and her family's leads to surprising snafus in their courtship. A touching, humorous love story from Kathleen, who is making her debut with us. **DELILAH'S WEAK-**

(continued)

NESS is her second book. Her first, **DEMON LOVER,** came from another publisher and was very well received. We hope you'll give a big warm welcome to Kathleen as a LOVESWEPT author.

Take one winsome little boy who yearns for his big sister's happiness . . . now mix his fervent wishes with those of a great big strong handsome hunk of a doctor who's smitten with said sister . . . then add in a lovely skittish young woman whose shoulders are burdened with responsibilities . . . and you have the recipe for one of Fayrene Preston's most delicious romances ever! It's **FIRE IN THE RAIN,** LOVESWEPT #140. Emotionally wrenching and humorous by turns, **FIRE IN THE RAIN** will keep you rooting for every one of little Joey's prayers to be answered . . . while you are riveted by the wild attraction and dramatic problems that pull together and separate the beautiful Lanie and the devastatingly tender and magnetic Rand. When you've finished this romance I hope you will agree with us that it is most appropriately titled, that the sizzling love between Lanie and Rand could in fact start a **FIRE IN THE RAIN**.

We received glowing letters about Adrienne Staff's and Sally Goldenbaum's first two books, so we're sure you will be delighted to know they are back with **CRESCENDO,** LOVESWEPTS #141. In this dramatic and delightful romance the marvelous, big-hearted Ellen Farrell from **BANJO MAN** finds her true love at last—but in a man who couldn't be more different from her if he'd been born and raised on the moon! He is Armand Dante, a debonair world-famous symphony conductor . . . and target of the attentions of a score of glamorous ladies in high society as well as gossip columnists. Ellen is a simple woman and a hard working, dedicated nurse. Worlds apart, indeed, and how you'll relish the way the twains do meet in this charming tale!

And for a merry, merry May mix up (yes, I know, it's April) be sure to get **TROUBLE IN TRIPLICATE,** LOVESWEPT #142, by Barbara Boswell. The Post triplets are identical beauties and one of them has been involved with a Saxon man. When our heroine

Juliet takes up the cause of her heartbroken sister, she finds herself falling madly in love with the brother of the scoundrel who had done her triplet wrong. Hero Caine is enthralled with Juliet from the first. As the couple fights it out over their respective siblings, at last joining forces on a scheme to reunite them, they get trapped in their own romantic plot. Then, one night amid thunder storms and lightning, they discover a tempest brewing between them to rival the weather . . . and the stormy relationship of her sister and his brother. Another outrageously wonderful love story from Barbara Boswell!

Well, I may be a little confused about the calendar day, but I do know exactly what kind of day it's going to be for a romance reader like you when next month's LOVESWEPTs go on sale—a very good day for sure!

Warm regards,

Sincerely,

Carolyn Nichols

Carolyn Nichols
  Editor
LOVESWEPT
Bantam Books, Inc.
666 Fifth Avenue
New York, NY 10103

LOVESWEPT

Love Stories you'll never forget by authors you'll always remember

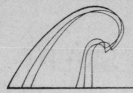 # LOVESWEPT

Love Stories you'll never forget by authors you'll always remember

☐	21708	**Out of This World** #103 Nancy Holder	$2.25
☐	21699	**Rachel's Confession** #107 Fayrene Preston	$2.25
☐	21716	**A Tough Act to Follow** #108 Billie Green	$2.25
☐	21718	**Come As You Are** #109 Laurien Berenson	$2.25
☐	21719	**Sunlight's Promise** #110 Joan Elliott Pickart	$2.25
☐	21726	**Dear Mitt** #111 Sara Orwig	$2.25
☐	21729	**Birds Of A Feather** #112 Peggy Web	$2.25
☐	21727	**A Matter of Magic** #113 Linda Hampton	$2.25
☐	21728	**Rainbow's Angel** #114 Joan Elliott Pickart	$2.25

Prices and availability subject to change without notice.

Buy them at your local bookstore or use this handy coupon for ordering: